When We Were Sane

A.H. King

This book is a work of fiction. References to real people, events, establishments, organizations or locales are intended only to provide a sense of authenticity and are used fictitiously. All other names, characters, businesses, events and incidents portrayed in this production other than those in the public domain are fictitious and a product of the author's imagination. No identification with actual persons (living or deceased), places, buildings, and products is intended or should be inferred.

Book Cover by Kim at KBG Designs

Editing by Brittany Bookworm Editing

Formatting made on Atticus

First edition 2024

AUTHOR'S NOTE

Dear Romantic Readers...

This is a fictional story about the madness that is love, set back in a time that was harsh on the post war mental health population. In this book, you'll find many truths of the era, but the story of Kasper and Ada would have looked a little different had it been truly from the times. However, the wonderful thing about writing is that it gets to be from my imagination, so please take this information for what it is. Love is the most powerful thing in the world and can show up in the least likely of hearts.

This book is not without trigger warnings. There are themes of the darker nature including war, bodily injury, death, mental illness, sexually explicit scenes, stalking, rape, suicide, violence and may not be suitable for all readers. You've been warned.

A.H. King

Dedication

To those who escape within our minds,
if only to experience the insanity of love...

PART I

Prologue - The End

Kasper

July 9th 1944

Death became me, buried beneath the rubble. The realization that there was no one coming to save me should have left me in despair, but I held no grudges. Everyone was fighting for their own lives; the enemy amongst us, doing the same. It was chaos until it wasn't. The last explosion hit above me as waves of fear turned into a quiet eeriness. The ringing in my ears and deafening silence that followed gave way to a moment of peace where I accepted that my time would be up, like an hourglass on its final grains of sand.

I became familiar with the taste of death over the years. It was part of what helped me survive. I knew the only way to remain alive was by separating my body from my mind, which can be easier said than done while witnessing the shooting of rapid fire around the grounds of where I stood. I'd watch my mates fall– sometimes several at a time to the earth below my feet. I could only stare helplessly at their bodies writhing in pain, begging for their mothers or laying in stillness for their souls to be collected in the slumber of the grim reaper. To survive was to become numb to the pain, regardless of whose it was. Now it's mine.

The village we found ourselves in today was a small means to the ending we were hoping to make of this operation. There was no mercy from the enemy, the framework of their loyalty disillusioned by power hungry men in their fatherland who sent them to fight and die the same as us. I couldn't entirely blame them, not the average man at least who, like me, was pulled into this war out of obligation to their country. Some of us bastards were lucky to have survived as long as we have. I shouldn't be alive and soon I won't be. I'll be like all the others: buried in a foreign land with a cross set up bearing my name back home in some field filled with the same simple crosses surrounding me. Strangers will glance at my name while they walk down the rows to find their loved ones and that will be all the acknowledgement my death will have. I have nothing to lose, and nothing to live for. I have no one to return to after all this. The friends I joined with are long dead. My family are nothing but decomposing bodies in the ground somewhere on this God forsaken earth. I have no woman to curl up in bed with and wake me from my nightmares. I accepted that this would be my fate and now it's come. There are no flashbacks of the bright memories I lived. There were none to begin with. There's only the feeling of contentment that comes with knowing I no longer have to live in hell, that this game is finally over and I can rest.

The dust covers my eyes and I no longer have the energy to open them. There's no pain. There's nothing except a warmth that spreads over my body like a wool blanket that's been heating up beside a fire, and I submit to the dreams that follow. The sounds of a forest, birds– fucking birds that I haven't yet heard in this hallowed land – pull at my senses. I see them in my subconscious, jumping from branch to branch and I stare down at my own body, bloody and broken, my face nearly unrecognizable. But somehow

I know it's me. There's so much blood, so much Goddamn blood everywhere, puddling beneath my soulless body. I hope they burn me. I never wanted to be buried, my remains stuck inside the dirt until the next generation digs me up when they build some city in these decimated parts. Burn my body and scatter my ashes, but don't fucking bury me in this country of horror. But they will, because it's the way things are done, like they are doing me a favour by honouring me in the dirt.

I look back up at the birds, so oblivious to the destruction around them. Or maybe they're not. Maybe they know. A little sparrow stares at me like it knows I still exist. I feel a sudden shooting pain run down my spine unlike anything I've ever felt, and my vision becomes dotted and unfocused. This must be it, the end.

CHAPTER 1

Kasper

JULY 11TH 1944

The beginning. That's what I tell myself when I wake up in a makeshift hospital bed to a woman changing my bandages. This is hell. The pain, it's fucking with me. I'm not supposed to feel it. I'm supposed to be dead. Maybe my soul is too fragile to travel to heaven. Maybe I don't belong there anymore. Or maybe it's some sick joke by the Gods to continue having me as a pawn in their game. I can barely take a deep breath and when I do, it feels like I'm being crushed by the cement pillars I walked through just hours ago. Or days. I don't know how long it's been.

"I'm Nurse Parsons. You've had an awful time at it, haven't you?"

I can't speak coherently. The only thing that escapes from my attempts are mumbles of pain that resemble the same suffering I've become accustomed to hearing over the years.

"We're going to get you all fixed up. You need to get some rest."

Like I'm supposed to do that when I am in absolute agony.

"We're running low, but this should help hopefully. Supplies should be coming soon."

She injects something into my thigh and everything soon goes black. I prefer that to being awake. I'd rather not wake at all.

I'm groggy when the night is over and the medicine has worn off. I look to my right to see a man in the bed beside me looking at a picture. He looks over at me and notices my stare.

"What a mess we've gotten ourselves into, eh mate?" he says in a weakened voice.

I don't reply.

"See this?" He turns the black and white picture to show me a beautiful woman with dark hair and a smile that could hypnotize any man.

"This is all I have of her. To think of spending my days in a chair when I should be taking care of her. Awful burden we are, aren't we? But that's not the hard part. The hard part is trying to get things back to the way they used to be before all this. Some days, I'd rather take a bullet to the head."

He looks at me and doesn't move for a moment, just stares me up and down, taking me in. Then he starts laughing. "I bet you wish you had that bullet too. Let me help to keep your mind off of –" he pauses, giving me a look of pity before continuing. "I've been away from her for some time now. But I never forget the softness of her hair, or the golden brown hues of her eyes. I never could tear my gaze away from them. I still see their depths when I sleep. She was... is the most wonderful precious thing. A spit fire she was when I first met her, and never a dull moment to be had. Always catching her in her daydreams. She'd sometimes dress up for me when I got home in these silk and chiffon night dresses that showed every curve of her body. Those were the days before Britain fell apart. Before we fell apart. You got a girl?"

He waits for my response and since I can't move my neck much to shake it no, or get any words out, I shut my eyes tight. I don't have anyone. I don't even remember the last time I was inside a woman.

"Well, maybe it's better off that way. No one to disappoint when we get out of here. To think I volunteered for this job. Thought I'd have a good story or two.

"My girl, she sure is something. Parents weren't very happy with me marrying her, you know, with her money situation and all, but it didn't matter. She was my second wife. First one died of tuberculosis. Shame. She was a good woman too. How lucky am I to experience two loves in one life? And gosh to think, if my first wife hadn't passed, I'd have never met this fire cracker of a woman." He taps the picture in his hand. "She put me through the ringer, this one. Beautiful and crazy."

The nurse comes back and pulls off the man's bed sheets. He's missing both of his legs.

"Ok Mr. Thompson, time to change your bandages and get some food into you."

I turn my attention away from him and stare up. We must be in a church, guessing by the stained glass windows and high arched ceilings with the large cross at the back that I can just make out in my periphery. The Gods, if there are Gods, sure have a sense of humour. Maybe there's one being in the sky making all the decisions or perhaps a counsel of figures that vote on our fates. I've never been one for organized religion, but I don't doubt there's something out there pulling strings. If only they could be pulled tight enough to strangle me and end this. If I say any prayer tonight, that's what it'll be for.

***

"NO! Don't shoot! HELP! Help me!" I hear a man yell in the distance, awakening from his night terrors. I can't move to see the commotion, but it's not the first night this has happened. Some are lulled to sleep by the sandman and the rest listen to the hysteria fill the room as men yell for their loved ones, reliving their worst moments. I look beside me at the man with no legs, the one who was talking to me just hours ago. He's becoming restless in his sleep, perhaps subconsciously being disturbed by the commotion. I try to fall back asleep myself, but it's no use. The pain is sliding up my spine once again, constricting my breath with each intake.

As the nurses are focused on the man across the room, I hear a gurgling sound coming from beside me. I turn my eyes and see my legless neighbour seizing uncontrollably. There's blood coming out of his mouth and nose, and I can't yell on his behalf. I try, but it's overshadowed by the noise coming from the other side of the room. His arm drops to the side of the bed, the seizing stops, and the blood from his mouth runs down the mattress and onto the floor, falling on top of the picture he once held. *Drip, drip, drip.*

Someone comes to help, but it's too late. It's always too late. After the doctor announces his death, his body is carried away, leaving the mess to be cleaned up by a younger nurse I haven't seen before. "Oh dear, sorry sir, it seems you dropped this." She places the picture in my hand and gets back to the mess beside me. I move my arm slightly to stare at the photo of the woman in my palm. One more widow. How many more would be made from the room of men I lay in?

Chapter 2

Ada

Present Day | July 14th 1947

This world was not made for the weak. A widow at thirty-eight isn't so typical around these parts. It somehow makes me feel more a part of a community and yet more alone than ever. Back before the war, if you were widowed, a rare occurrence with any woman under forty where I come from, you were given special attention. Maybe you'd become the talk around the town or have a bloke or two delivering flowers to your door for your next chance at love. But now, it's like I just mix in with everyone else; this itself is contradictory, because though I know a few just like me, it's a lonely place to be.

"Kiddo, can you go into my room for me and grab the envelope on my desk?" My father says as he adjusts his large body on the worn couch beneath him. It doesn't matter the age. He'll always call me kiddo, the same as he did when I was a child.

Injured in the first war, my father got around with the help of a walking stick. One bad hip and a lifetime's worth of factory work, and the man is barely standing these days. It's my job to take care of him now.

To be honest, I hate this house; the one I was born in and the one I'll probably die in. I came back here even before I found out Edward had been killed. Our London flat we had was blown to bits during the night raids. I was lucky enough to be visiting my father that evening, or I would have been amongst the fire that burned into the night.

My little job at the grocers was a taxing position at the time, with the locals trying to get in my favour to enlarge their portions. But my perspective started to change as the blitz continued; the men continued to leave and there were little comforts left.

The past casts a shadow on me even now. I wish I had done more. We all became different people, but at least others did something noble. I had nothing to complain about at all really. Not until the post arrived that fateful day.

Edward came from a good family. A wealthy one at that, and though I never married him for his money, I knew I would benefit from it. He seemed like a good man at first, infatuated with the little grocer. I was practically a crone at twenty-eight when he asked me for dinner. My father had been asking me at every dinner when I would find a man to settle down with. So it only made sense to accept Edward's proposal when the time came. To be honest, when he left for the war, it didn't feel much different. He was a busy man, one who loved me dearly, and I was grateful his hand was kind. I never thought I would be getting a letter. He was a journalist, not a soldier. But the wrong place at the wrong time made casualties of even regular men.

His death gave me a small cushion of insurance money, but his family made sure I didn't see anything else. Even then, the money has gone to helping us stay afloat.

I hand my father the envelope, or at least I try to, but he pushes it back in my hand.

"It's been a while since we've talked about your mother. You should think about visiting her."

"I'd really rather not," I reply.

"Well, your choice I suppose. But you should read this and then decide." The envelope looks yellowed and dated and has been folded in half.

"Your mother wrote this for you. It was a long time ago. She said I should give it to you when you turned into a woman and well, to be honest, I forgot about it. I know we've been having some bad days lately, and I found this and I just thought you might want to get some of that closure you've talked about. I don't know what she wrote, but if it helps in any way, read it."

I hadn't seen my mother for many years. I don't often go visit her, and for good reason. I think I'm doing her a favour by staying away.

As I said, I was born in this house, in the kitchen I walk through each day. My father delivered me himself with my mother not trusting the midwife who was supposed to be here for my birth. My mother was convinced she would only do harm. She said she saw the devil in her. I was a twin, the first born, and my brother, who they named Corbin, was born lifeless shortly after me. She blamed me, saying I killed him in the womb. My father only saw me as the miracle that survived.

Over the years, my mother's grudge towards me got worse and her mental state even more so. She tried to kill me a couple times, saying I was a demon of sorts. I was four when my father caught my mother trying to smother me with a pillow the first time. I was six when she decided a knife would be a better solution. My father stopped her and got her help. Hysteria, they called it. She lives at the Huberts

Home Asylum for the mentally ill, a psychiatric institution that she's been at since.

My father watches me closely, I think hoping that I won't turn into her. I don't tell him about my dreams, or the shadows I see hiding in the corner of my room sometimes, or how I knew my husband was dead before we got the notice. My mother is nothing but an empty shell now, nothing good of her remaining. The treatments have caused her to be calm at least, but her brain is desolate of any real thoughts. I won't risk ending up like her. I'd rather have an abundance of thoughts than none at all, no matter how scattered my mind feels on most days.

"I'll read it. Thank you," I respond.

I head to my room, the larger one my father used to share with my mother that he insisted I take. I sit on the small stool by my vanity and look in the oval mirror. I wear a dulled burnt orange day dress with a back tie that tightens at my waist with a modest v-neck. Over it, I throw on my knit cream cardigan that has a hole in the back shoulder. I've sewn it nearly three times now. It doesn't matter how tight I thread it, it always seems to come loose. I draw closer to the mirror, noticing the lines on the outside of my honey brown eyes, and my thick auburn hair, the natural red from my fathers side of the family looking more drab today than usual. I don't have much of my mother's looks. I'm grateful for the lack of reminder when I look at myself. My mother's frame is small, and her hair the darkest brown, next to black, with natural waves that I wish I did inherit. Mine is thick and straight, only curled by pin curls that I have to do each night for it to stay for an entire day. My hips are much wider, and I always wear the right dress to shrink my waist so as to not bring notice to them. Perhaps it's a good thing I can't afford to buy anything new. It gives me an excuse to wear my old fashions. Even as worn as they are, they suit me.

I hold the envelope in my hand and open it reluctantly. My mothers handwriting is sloppy and doesn't stay centered on the yellowed paper. It smells like my fathers tobacco and I see my name at the top with the date, realizing I was only still a child when she wrote this.

Dec 24th 1916
Ada,
I pondered what to write in this letter for the last couple of months. I'm not one for words, but I need you to know a few things while my head is still clear enough to express these growing thoughts. I loved you once, when you were kicking inside of me. I loved you before I met you and I loved you briefly, for the short period of time you breathed air before Corbin. But Corbin's death meant the death of the love I thought I had for you. You stole him from me, his life and mine. The truth is I can't love you without hating myself and without betraying my son. So I'm giving you this final letter to let me go. Please forget about me as I will of you. I never felt like your mother, and I know it's because I was never meant to be. I hope you can one day make amends for the life you stole. Plead your case with God and you may save your soul.

-Helen

That hurt more than I thought. I wonder if my father would have given me this letter had he known the contents of it. It makes sense now though. Helen never looked at me with any affection. She wouldn't take her eyes off my father, but I was ignored, which seems to be a common theme in my life. How sad. Is it pathetic to have pity for myself for a moment? I rip up the letter in little pieces and toss them into a nearby waste bin.

"Ada," I hear a whisper in my ear and turn, but there's nothing there.

I walk to the door to peek out into the hallway "Father, did you say something?" I hear nothing.

I feel a coldness caress my skin like the aftermath of a storm. I tighten my cardigan into my chest and pick up my latest book, *Poems by Lord Byron.* I cuddle up on my bed, grateful the day is over and just as I'm drifting into an evening slumber, I'm startled by my name being said again. "Ada."

Fuckin' hell.

I walk down the hall and find my father asleep back on the couch in his usual spot.

Right, it's been a long day and I must be tired. My mother's letter must be getting to me. I walk into the kitchen that is separated by a serving hatch and reach under the sink where I know my father hides his gin. I pour myself a small glass and down in it straight, hoping that will be enough to lull me to sleep. Just in case, I pour another and walk back to my room. It still feels cooler than the rest of the house, which is odd in the heat of the summer. I don't complain because I'll take this reprieve from the July heat even if it's temporary. I finish reading the poem *When We Two Parted* by Lord Byron.

In secret we met —
In silence I grieve,

That thy heart could forget,
They spirit deceive.
If I should meet thee
After long years,
How should I greet thee? —
With silence and tears.

And just as I get to the last line, I surrender to the gin and fall asleep.

CHAPTER 3

Ada

Sunday mornings are always my favourite time of the week. Everyone's off to church, while I get to take my time sleeping in and enjoying a slow breakfast. Church was never really welcoming for me. I used to go to Sunday mass with Edward, but there was always gossip that made its rounds, and the whispers I would hear of my mother's history confirmed that I wasn't to be accepted in the house of God.

I prepare myself and my father breakfast and wonder why he isn't awake yet. I peek into his room to see him sitting at his desk slumped over.

"Father, are you alright?"

"Ada, I'm afraid I'm under the weather today. Would you mind running down and grabbing some tea? I think that might just be the thing to help."

"Of course," I say with a look of concern.

Sal's General Store that I work at is always open on Sunday afternoons for a few hours for the church ladies to stop by if they need extras for dinner.

Our 1938 navy blue Ford Sedan is in need of repairs so instead of driving, I walk. Sal's isn't far, and I don't mind the exercise. My mother's letter is playing in my head, and I'm trying my best to distract myself with the outside views. It's a perfectly cloudy day, where the shapes change as quick as the wind passes.

The store is practically empty when I arrive. I don't normally do my shopping on Sunday's, but I'll pick up a few extra things while I'm here.

The store itself is small and quaint, and even with some local competition, we've remained in business due to the loyalty of Max's customers. Sal was his father who passed on the family business to Max before he died. Though it has evolved over the years, the store was a reliable producer of goods during the war and remains so with rationing still in place. Those who were around during the most difficult of times never forgot it.

There's a counter at the back with canned goods and cereals, and fresh fruit and vegetables are gathered in baskets towards the front of the store. I walk over to the peaches and start looking through them.

Peaches are just coming into season, and these are much different than the tinned peaches we lived off of for some time. They have always been my favourite fruit. I hold onto the peach in my hand, studying the soft skin and firmness. This one looks perfect, but I don't take it. I put it back down and grab the one next to it. It's bruised on one spot, softened by the damage, and hard everywhere else. I hold onto it longer, examining the fruit before I place it in my hand basket. I grab another peach, this one perfectly round with an even stem. I place it back in the basket and instead choose one buried underneath, which is misshapen, dented and a bit sticky from the juice it had leaked. I put it next to the one I already picked. I grab a third peach from the front where we all know everyone touches but never takes. It's been handled over and over again, and the peach itself is far more pale than the rest. I bring it up to my nose to smell and I get nothing. I place it in the basket.

"I hope your other choices in life are a bit more thought out than the peaches you just picked," a deep voice says beside me. I see him in my peripheral vision but I don't look at him. I just stand there, staring down at the peaches.

"Who's to say those damaged peaches aren't just as good as these other perfect looking ones? Why should they be left to rot just because they're different? They deserve love too. Plus we all know peaches don't taste really good until August. These are just a tease. A few more weeks and these will be much better." I turn to walk to the barrel of potatoes nearby as I feel eyes on me.

"Why don't you wait until August? Why settle for something you won't be satisfied with?"

I turn towards him and am awestruck with how handsome this man in front of me is. He's got dark blond hair, combed back slightly to the side, with the front gently tousled to hang over the side of his forehead. He wears brown slacks and a white button up shirt rolled up to his elbows and a diagonally striped tie around the collar. He looks like he belongs in an ad. His eyes are the kind of blue that entirely contrast with his darker eyelashes, the kind any woman would be envious of, making his eyes pop out even more. The depths of them suck me in until I notice his full lips and sharp cheekbones on his clean shaven face that feel intimidating to be in the same room as. He's got crows feet around his eyes, showing his days gone by. Though he's a stranger to me in every way, something about him feels familiar.

I take a deep breath, gathering my thoughts before letting myself speak in the presence of such a man. "Because maybe I won't be here in August. None of us are guaranteed our next breath. So I'll settle for damaged peaches in July, and when August comes, I'll enjoy them that much more."

I grab a few potatoes and place them in my basket, heading over to where the fresh loaves of baked brown bread have been placed.

"Are you following me?" I reluctantly ask.

"Yes."

I wasn't expecting that blunt of an answer, but here we are.

"And that would be because?"

He leans over to look into my very sparse basket and grabs the first damaged peach that I picked out from the barrel. He holds it in his large hand, making the peach look miniature in comparison, and takes a bite out of it without breaking eye contact with me. "Mmm, not bad."

"I was going to eat that."

"Maybe. Or you might have let it sit in your fruit bowl collecting fruit flies until you decided it was time to feed it to the dogs. I, on the other hand, don't waste time in eating my way through the sweet damage, right to the core. It's a good peach."

"Well then please, help yourself to the others. And I don't have dogs," I smirk with annoyance.

He laughs breathily. "How about you let me take you out and we can enjoy one together. Maybe a walk in the gardens. How do you feel about a film?"

"Or, how about you let me finish shopping and find someone else's peaches to steal."

"I'll take the first option."

I don't know what he thinks he's doing. His ego is either entirely inflated and he's looking for some innocent little thing to make it even bigger, or he's a gorgeous killer looking for his next vulnerable victim. Either way, I'm not taking the bait.

"There's a woman that just walked by the shop with black hair. She couldn't seem to take her eyes off of you. I'm sure she'd be ever so grateful for a night out."

He doesn't break his gaze away from me even for a second's glimpse.

"What's your name?"

"None of your business."

His smile reaches up to his eyes and his brows lift slightly. "Your name?" he persistently asks again.

"What use is my name when you'll never need to use it again?"

"I need to know what name I should use when I'm thinking about you tonight."

Well that was highly inappropriate. Does this man think I'm a lonely harlot? "Does that line work for you?"

"I don't know. I've never used it. You tell me."

I start to walk away to head to the cash where Max is working.

"My name is Elaina, okay? Now can you go?"

He stops beside me as I approach Max.

"Can't get enough of this place, can you Ada?" Max says.

"Oh well, you know me, always forgetting things like the silly woman I am. I need some tea while I'm here too."

"I knew you didn't look like an Elaina. And besides, I can tell you're lying. Your neck is flushed and your breathing is a little rapid."

"Maybe because there's a strange man following me around in the grocery store at noon on a Sunday."

Max's eyes dart to the man and then back to me.

The man leans over and whispers, "Baby, you think I'm strange now, wait till you get to know me."

"Well, that won't be happening."

I ask Max for a portion of butter, then go to hand him the cash from my purse when I realize I must have forgotten it. My money pouch is empty and I feel the flush of my face deepen with embarrassment.

"Don't worry Ada, I'll put it on your tab," Max assures me.

The stranger analyzes my face for a second, and I suppose he must like what he sees because he smiles with his teeth, then drops his gaze to my lips. His eyes darken when he returns them to me and it sets me on edge.

"Goodbye for now, *Ada,*" he says, emphasizing my name while taking another bite from the peach as he walks away.

A man of dreams and nightmares, no doubt. I brush off the strange occurrence and head back home. A blessing in disguise, perhaps, because it got my mother's letter off my mind, if only for the moment.

CHAPTER 4

Kasper

She's as gorgeous as her picture. No, more. Older than in the photo, but beautiful nonetheless. It's been three years since I died. Three. I thought I knew hell, but hell was spent in those days after the battle. The physical pain was blinding. But the mental pain, the images that kept me from my sleep, those were worse. For the first time in years, I had been safe, warm, dry, away from the danger, and it was during those early days when I was separated from it all that I felt the most vulnerable. I had time to think, and time is what I didn't want. I wanted a distraction, but I had nothing to do except heal my body along with my mind. If I couldn't fix what was inside my head, what good would I be to her?

I spent the better part of the next three years trying to get my life back in order, taking temporary jobs as they came up. And when the time was right, I got the position I needed and found a small flat nearby.

More than half the men I once worked with in my old life were gone, and the days seemed to drag on with no end in sight. But each night I went to bed, I looked at her picture, my beauty, with dried blood still reminding me of our origins on that fateful night. She was put into my hand for a reason.

I wondered what she was doing with her life. A good looking woman like her would surely have been scooped up, maybe remarried. She was the only hope I had to the outside world, that maybe I'd get lucky enough one day and meet someone that I could love just the same. But there was no one. She was my hope. She was my survival. She was my brief reprieve from my long days, looking at her picture, imagining our life together.

"Kas, tell me why are you doing this? We've been happy, haven't we?" My bleak little whore tries to convince me.

"If by happy, you mean my cock has been satisfied for the last couple of years, then yes, Joan, we've been happy. But I can't see you any more."

Joan was a beautiful woman but didn't even hold a candle to Ada. We met at a pub once and would meet up from time to time to fulfill each other's needs. A needy little fuck she was, but it was never serious.

"Just tell me why. I know Theo and I are starting to court, but it doesn't mean we can't still see each other in the meantime. I'm not even sure he's right for me."

"I've met someone, someone I'm quite serious about. And Theo is a good man, Joan. You'd be silly not to marry someone like him. I'm damaged goods, and I need someone who understands that part of me."

Joan was in her late twenties, a governmental secretary that had turned down six proposals, all for the chance to be someone in office. A woman of ambition, she avoided marriage. The war gave women the opportunity to step into roles they might not have been able to otherwise.

"Oh, but perhaps just once more. It's been months after all. Can't we just– one more time?" She places her one hand on my shoulder and the other stroking my chest, drifting it down towards my belt. I grab her wrist in response.

"I'm a faithful man, my dear. I can't in good conscience have anything more to do with you. You'll need to leave now, Joan."

I walk over to the door and open it for her, waiting for her to leave, and she does, sulkingly while she looks down to the floor.

"You'll come back to me. You always do. You just need to miss me a little first," she says.

I close the door behind her.

Now to plan how I will get Ada to fall in love with me.

CHAPTER 5

Ada

"Max, I can't! I won't! I'm not ready."

"Of course you are. Give him a chance. Just once. If you don't hit it off, I'll never mention it again."

Max has been trying to set me up with his neighbour named Troy. What kind of name is Troy anyway?

"One time Max, and that's it."

"Excellent! He's a good guy to talk to. Trust me," he says, while I finish stocking the side shelves with new products.

Max reminds me of my Grandfather from my father's side who passed away when I was young. He's a larger man, like my father, with a great big belly, grey hair, a beard that wraps around his face and a larger mustache filling in the gaps.

I hear the bells ringing but I'm preoccupied in helping Mrs. Bentley.

"Ms. Thompson, it's good to see you. I was hoping to have some of your peach chutney that you put out each year."

"A couple more weeks. I'll be sure to put aside a jar for you."

"Oh two please, would you! Me and Malcom will fight over it otherwise."

I giggle. "Yes, of course. Why don't I drop it off to you once I've made it."

"Oh thank you dear, that would be lovely. You have a good day now."

I watch her leave and notice a tall man standing behind her. *Now where did he come from?*

"Will you save a jar of peach chutney for me as well?" The man asks. "Oh Ada, we have to stop meeting like this," he smiles.

"I'm working. Please leave."

"Well, I'm here as a customer. For now."

"What would you like?"

"Aren't you going to ask me my name?"

"I don't need to know your name. I just need to know what you want."

"I want you, darling. How's that sound? Would you wrap yourself up for me, tie a pretty bow around you?"

I blush and try to look away to hide it but no doubt he notices.

"Good news Ada, Troy is going to meet you at 5:00."

"Oh, but I work until 6:00."

"Not tonight you don't. He'll come get you from here."

I have nothing to wear but my work dress. Maybe it's a good thing. It'll scare him off to see how dreadful I look in this worn outfit. I don't have the heart to tell Max that I really need the money more than this date.

"Okay, Max, but if this doesn't go well, you'll owe me."

"And if it does, you'll thank me," he taps me on the nose.

"Do you have a date, Ada?"

Max chimes in, "You could say that. The guy is quite charming if I do say so myself. A little more grey in the hair mind you, but a good man. Ada could use the company."

The man looks like he's going to be sick. His eyes speak of terrible things and he fists his right hand in a tight ball, causing his knuckles to turn white.

"Is that right *Max?*"

Max looks concerned for a moment, then the man looks back at me and puts on a fake smile. "Well, enjoy your company."

He leaves without uttering another word. I have the feeling this won't be the last time I see him.

***

The date was more than awful. It was atrocious. I've had more fun serving food to hungry, war wrecked women pining for rations than sitting at this date. His breath smelled like whisky, and at first I tried to give him the benefit of the doubt. Perhaps he was nervous, and I can't blame him for that, but he was a smug bastard whose intellectuals belittled my lack of education. He made me feel small, then ignored me for a beautiful blond across the room. I got out of there as soon as my food was done, stating an illness coming on. I think he even believed me.

I fiddle with my purse, looking for my keys for a moment outside of my house. In my state of distraction, I don't notice the man blocking my door.

"Oh for Christ's sake," I spit out.

"What a foul little mouth you have," he says, his lips turning up at me.

"I'm not in the mood, stranger. Please leave."

"By now, we're hardly strangers, Ada."

"Well, you are to me. I don't even know your name."

"That's because you didn't want to know. It's Kasper, by the way. And how was your date?"

"Absolutely dreadful if you must know. I would much appreciate this night to be over."

I push Kasper aside, grabbing for the door handle and notice it's open. Thank goodness my father left it unlocked, because my keys are nowhere to be found. It's been that kind of day apparently. However, Kasper puts his hand overtop of mine on the door handle, pulling it closed. I turn to him, his face only inches away from mine as he cages me in with one hand on each side of me.

He looks around, likely to make sure no one is watching. Leaning into my ear, he says deeply, "No more dates. Not unless they are with me. I wanna know you, piece by piece. Tell me, what makes you wild, feral? What makes those knickers of yours wet? What makes you tick, dear Ada, my little peach."

I can't move or breathe, and there's something going on with my body that has been comatose for many years.

"I think you should leave now."

"For now."

He walks away and I quickly get in the house. My father must be asleep. That's early, even for him. I turn on the radio broadcast and head to my wardrobe to find some more comfortable clothing that I lay out on my bed. That's when I notice it. Sitting on my nightstand is the book *Wuthering Heights* by Emily Bronte. I open it up and on the inside page is a handwritten message.

I long for the day to hold you tight,
Through every sleepless night.
For if I am to fall asleep,
I'll lose you from my sight.

From your adherent admirer

My father must have put this here; maybe it is an old book that he found. Someone must have written that poem for a loved one. He is still not feeling well and he had to postpone his visit to Huberts, but maybe that's for the best. He's always down for a few days after he sees her anyway, and I hate seeing him like that. I know he loves her, but I never understood how. A man and a wife love each other out of obligation, not anything more than that.

My room cools again and I grab my cardigan. Such strange July weather we are having. I go grab a towel from the closet to take a bath. Tonight I'll wash my hair and set it overnight.

As I open the closet door from the hallway, I hear music playing. It's a familiar sound, and I follow it down the hall. Then it stops. I listen for a moment longer. Perhaps I didn't hear anything at all. Maybe my father put something on the tele. But then I hear it again. It's coming from my room. There's an eerie presence in my room, as if I'm being watched. The music is coming from my wardrobe. I open the door and grab the old shoe box that's hidden at the back of the top shelf and place it on my bed. When I open it, I pull out the small music box that Edward gave me for our anniversary. Inside of it, I keep my wedding ring. I haven't worn it since his funeral, the one we threw without his body. How strange that it plays music after being quiet for so long. It must be broken. I take out the music box, watching it, trying to find where the sound comes from, but it has stopped and I can't find its origin. I place it on my bed and wait a few minutes, but when nothing plays, I put it back in the box and place it back in my wardrobe.

I leave the distraction behind, enjoying my bath, taking extra time to soak in it. It's warm and refreshing at the same time if there's such a thing. It's absolutely glorious and I clear my mind, devoiding it of any worries, at least for a moment. That is until I picture him, my handsome stranger. I don't understand how a man of his stature and looks would even try and take out a woman like me. I'm practically a hag at my age, widowed, working at a local grocer, living with my father. It was already a miracle when Edward fell for me. But things like this don't happen twice. Yet, I dare to wonder how good it would feel to be with another man.

I run my hand slowly down my breast and into the warmth of the water until I reach the parts of me that are reacting to these thoughts. Edward used to call it his honey pot and I did enjoy my time with him in the evenings. It's been so long that I probably have cobwebs down there now. I begin rubbing myself up and down at first, but then change to a circling rhythm. My cheeks heat as I start to picture Kasper being the one to touch me. I wonder how it would feel. The sensation intensifies.

"You almost done in there?" my father calls in.

And it's gone. I guess he's not asleep.

"I'll be right out."

He doesn't say anything else, but it's too late. I can't get back there now. Then I feel the shame come on. *What was I thinking?*

After my hair is set in pin curls and I've gotten into bed, I feel a pull, like someone has just tugged on my blanket. I look up in the dark but see nothing. I reach over and turn on my light. Perhaps my blanket just got snagged on the bed.

I reluctantly get out of bed and walk to my fathers room. I look over to the bed at him sleeping peacefully. "Love you old man," I whisper.

I head back to bed and shut my light off again.

***

The morning comes before I know it. I slept through the night, which is a rarity for me.

I go to make my father breakfast and get ready for work. To my surprise he's not awake yet, and his morning paper has arrived. I go to bring him a fresh cup of tea in bed instead to go with his paper and forego the breakfast until his appetite is ready. When I walk in the room, he's still sleeping. He's been sleeping a lot lately.

"Father, I've brought you a tea and your paper. I'll just leave it here." I place it beside his bed and gently touch his arm. His arm is cold. I pull the blanket down just enough to see his full face and he's pale, his lips holding a bluish tinge.

I shake him, "Father." I shake him harder, "Father!" I tap him on the face. "Father! Wake up!" Panic starts to rise, bile moving up my throat and I place both my hands on his face, turning him toward me. I stare down in shock trying to comprehend what I'm seeing.

I run outside and yell desperately for help. My neighbour comes running dressed in her work uniform, likely on the way herself.

"Please!" I beg "It's my father. He's not waking up. We need an ambulance." My neighbour addresses another passerby to call for help and follows me into where he is lying.

"I need you to wake him up. He's had a headache, you see. I tried to give him a hot drink but he hasn't woken up and well, he's so cold. We have to warm him up. You must have something for him."

"I'm sorry mam but he's gone. There's no pulse."

"Well that can't be. He was fine just last night. Just a headache. He's fine. He just needs to be warmed up and given some medicine. A tea would help. He loves tea. Surely you have something else to help him."

"There's nothing we can do. He's no longer here. We'll call the coroner."

I fall to the ground and plead with God to bring him back. I don't have anyone else. He was it. I can't lose him.

The woman puts her hand on my shoulder, and I start sobbing uncontrollably. I feel like I'm about to throw up. I can't lose anyone else. I feel like I'm about to collapse; my vision goes blurry, my breath quickens and everything goes black.

CHAPTER 6

Ada

She stares at a blank wall in the small beige room we've been given to have our visitation. Helen barely moves these days; my father had said she's been having a hard time.

"The funeral was nice. A lot of people from his old job came to say their goodbyes. I brought you this." I hold his favourite woolen jumper in my hand and pass it to her. She doesn't look at it. Just continues to stare.

"I thought you could have it, as a memory. Father would want you to have it. He loved you Helen, very much so. I'm sorry for your loss."

Just as I get up to leave, I hear movement behind me. "Demon," she growls while pointing at me. I don't know what to say in response, so I don't say anything. I just wait.

"You took them! YOU TOOK THEM! DEMON!" She drops her pointed finger and stares at me coldly in the eyes.

"I'm sorry for your loss, but you're wrong. I cared for him very much."

Helen reaches into her pocket and pulls out a knife. How the hell did she get that?

"Guard!" I yell, but it's too late.

She paces towards me, and just as I think she's about to lunge at me with the knife in hand, she smiles and slits her own throat, dropping to the floor just as the guard reaches her. There's yelling and commotion, but I can't do anything except stand there and watch as the blood pools by my heels. I bring my hand up to my face to feel blood dripping from it. My pale yellow dress is splotched with red, and that cold feeling comes over me again. I'm shivering without the goosebumps. I'm led out of the room and brought down the hall into an office.

"I don't understand," I say to the nurse that's comforting me.

"Here take this, it will help with your nerves." She hands me a pill and a cup of water. I don't even know when she had time to get that for me. How long have I been sitting here? I swallow the pill anyway and get lost staring out the small window. A shadow casts over me. When I look up, I see a tall man leaning against a desk in front of me.

"Hello, Ada. How are you feeling?"

I stare at him in disbelief. "Kasper?"

"You can call me that, yes. The staff here call me Dr. Knight."

"You work here?"

"I do, yes."

"Well, how is it that I've never seen you?" I ask, pondering this new information. Did he know that my mother was a patient here? Did he know of me before this?

"I'm new here. I worked at Bethlam before this."

"That's strange. Don't you think the chances of that are strange?"

"Very much so. We should talk about your mother."

"She's not my mother. Not anymore. She never was. She gave birth to me and that's it. They said she was having some unpredictable behavior lately. She was speaking of dark things, saying a man was coming for her. They tried to medicate her to help with the episodes, but they persisted I suppose. How did she get the knife?

Isn't there some sort of security protocol put in place? You should have checked her things." I'm quite furious with their negligence.

"I assure you, we're very thorough, but sometimes these things happen. Items are snuck in at visitations and traded for favours. These people may be demented, but that doesn't mean they aren't smart."

I can feel the medicine kick in, and a calmness sweeps over me. "I can't plan another funeral. Especially for a woman who resented my existence."

"What about your father? Do you want to tell me about him?"

I shake my head.

"The coroner will have to take her body for a proper autopsy report, given the circumstances of her death. Whatever she said to you, it wasn't your fault."

"My father wanted to be buried beside her and his plot is big enough for both of them. I don't think it was meant for me. I suppose I'd rather be turned into dust anyway. She should have it."

"We'll take care of it," he promises.

"This is too fresh. I need to get out. I need to leave. I'm sorry." I walk out of the room and just keep walking, my mind calmly buzzing with whatever they gave me.

Somehow I make it home, a little more dazed and breathless than before. Thankfully the asylum is only a short distance from where I reside. Father never did want to move for that reason. And yet I suddenly resent being in this house. I want to burn it to the ground and the memories along with it so I can move past this terrible, terrible month.

I pass out on the couch my father would normally be on, dried blood remaining all over me, and when I wake, it's the next day. I walk into the bathroom to clean myself up. I'm an absolute mess.

I turn the shower on and just as I'm about to walk in, I hear a bang. I wrap my house coat around me and open the bathroom door. I walk down the hall, further investigating the noise, and see a vase has fallen: my mother's vase, the one I refused to put flowers in. My father kept it on the mantle with dried flowers in it, so it wouldn't have to be replaced. They were old and dusty, and now they are crumbled, scattered bits on the ground, the vase in pieces. But that's not what gets my main attention. On the coffee table in front of the sofa, there's a book. A book that wasn't there minutes ago when I woke. I walk over and pick it up.

"Hello?" I yell out, in case anyone is here. I should be scared, but I'm too numb from the previous day's events to care. The book is titled *Rebecca* by Daphne du Maurier, and inside there's another handwritten poem on the inside page.

Stricken with the pain of a thousand wounds,
I too have felt death and surrendered to the streams of blood that followed.
For our wounds do not heal six feet under-ground,
Nor do they six feet above.
And the only remedy is the one we deny ourselves when we can't see past today.
Tomorrow will come,
In this life or another.

From Your Fated Love

The vase, the music box. Do I have a stalker or a ghost? Has he been going through my things? I'll need to change the locks. I lock the door to the bathroom and wash the blood off of me, staying longer than I should in the steam just to ease the tension. I get out, get dressed and head to the kitchen, grabbing the gin from under the sink. I plop down in front of the broken ceramic and pop off the top of the gin, downing gulp after gulp, gagging in between. Today's not the day to clean up the broken shards of my life. Today is the day to forget it all happened to begin with.

CHAPTER 7

Kasper

My broken beauty is even prettier covered in blood, just like her photo. I'll give her some time to grieve of course. How insensitive would I be if I seduced her so soon after her loss. She's like me, alone. I knew we were meant to be. I knew her picture was given to me for a reason. I knew there was a reason I survived when I shouldn't have. Had I gone mad in the days after the war, I would have been just like all the other men whose heads were clouded with their worst days. But she...she kept me from the endless cycle of reliving each day. She was the only thing that helped me sleep at night. All the times I've rubbed my cock to the site of that damn picture just to have some relief. Soon, she'll be rubbing it for me. But not yet. I have to give her time. I have to step away. But I won't let her believe she's alone. She'll never feel alone again.

"Dr. Knight, can you come with me please? There's a patient that needs to see you."

"What is it today?"

"It's Ms. Kensington. She's refusing to leave her bed again."

I walk down the corridor to the small grey painted room on the left. Ms. Kenzington has been a patient here for two years now after attempting to kill her husband. Frankly, I don't blame her. He had beaten her for years and she'd finally had enough. Poisoned his morning coffee, but got the dose wrong. He survived, then made sure she never saw freedom again.

"Ms. Kensington, how are we today?"

"Not good, doc. You see, I ran out of books to read and I know you had some good ones on your desk the last time I was in there and I was wondering if I might borrow one."

"The last time I gave you a book from my personal stash, I believe you tore out the pages and entertained yourself with paper airplanes. I don't wish for my literature to turn into an aerodynamics lesson in the ward."

"Please, I've read all the ones in the rec room. Surely you could give me another chance."

"Why don't I do you one better. How about some paper, so you can write your own stories. Wouldn't that be swell?"

"Well I never thought of such a thing, but I suppose I could give it a try. Maybe I could tell my story. Doctor Johnson— oh you don't know him. He was here before you. He went on stress leave and never came back. Anyway, he said I should find a means to get clear in the head with it all. I could even read it to you when I'm done. Then maybe they would believe me. Maybe they would even let me go. Do you think that's possible?"

"You've been declared insane for attempted murder, Ms. Kensington. Your time here ends when your sentence is over."

"I can't possibly survive much longer in here. It's ludicrous. He's out there with his pretty new wife while I'm in here decaying. How long before her bruises appear I wonder. I bet she'll be in here before I get out. Mark my words, Dr. Knight."

"I'll have one of the nurses bring you some writing materials tomorrow, and that's only if you agree to get out of bed today."

"Well fine. If this is your way of negotiating, then I must say you have your ways, doctor."

***

I finish up my shift and make my way back to my flat. Many of the staff stay on sight at a staff residence across the street, but I decided against it. I felt it was best to separate work from home as much as I could. Privacy is a luxury that I don't plan on giving up any day soon. When you've spent every night for four years laying beside your fellow men, the prospect of having a place just for you is alluring enough.

When I arrive at home, there's a familiar woman standing at the front gates of my building.

"Joan, what are you doing here?"

She holds her hand up and shows me the ring. "We're getting married, Kas. Isn't it wonderful?" The look on her face says otherwise.

"Wonderful Joanie. Give Theo my congratulations."

"That's just the thing. Theo is a good man. Any woman would be so proud to be his, but well, truthfully—" She pauses and paces slightly in her stance. "I'm in love with *you*. I always have been, I think. I think in time, you could love me too. Or perhaps you already do. We could be happy, couldn't we? I can give you everything you want. I know how you like your eggs in the morning and how you like to be pleased. I know your mind. I can't marry Theo if I know we have a chance."

I take her hand in my palm and cover it with my other, smiling softly at her. "You're a doll, Joan, but you don't know my mind, you only know my body. I don't love you, and I don't think I ever could. Not in the way you deserve to be loved. I told you, my heart belongs to someone else, and I plan on asking her to marry me. You need to go back home now. Go to Theo, plan your wedding. I'll even be there if you like."

She looks at me with somber eyes, tears clouding her vision but not yet released. "What did I do wrong?"

"You did nothing wrong. You gave me company when I needed it. You've been a good friend. But you and I both said from the beginning it was an arrangement and nothing more. And it's been nothing more for me."

Joan slaps me across the face and the tears fall down her soft pink cheeks.

"I regret the day I ever met you, Kas!" She storms off down the sidewalk, the sounds of her heels clicking on the cement, leaving small echoes behind on the empty street.

"Tough day?" a man leaving the building says to me, having been a witness to Joan's final words.

"You have no idea."

CHAPTER 8

Ada

It's been weeks since Helen's burial that I didn't attend. I dissolve into an empty house, the scent of death floating around my fathers room as if his body was still there, decomposing. But he's gone. This house feels as if I'm living under a curse. The noises have continued; sometimes footsteps that aren't there, sometimes a door left open that I could have sworn I closed. Just the other day, my wedding ring, the very ring I put back in the music box, was sitting on my nightstand. And as for my mystery books, there have been two more since the last, with poems handwritten in each. The first book was *Jane Eyre* by Charlotte Bronte.

I AM YOUR SHADOW AND YOUR SALVATION,
YOUR SANITY AND YOUR SPELL,
YOUR SOLITUDE AND YOUR SACRIFICE.
MASKING OUR GHOSTS WITHIN THESE CONFINES.
THE WHISPERS WE LEAVE BEHIND,
AS WE ESCAPE TO NEW WORLDS.

FROM YOUR DEVOTED DEVIANT

And the second poem, found inside a dictionary of all books.

NOT IN THESE PAGES IS LOVE DEFINED IN THE
WAY I FEEL FOR YOU,
FOR LOVE DOES NOT MEET OUR MATCH,
IT DOES NOT SPEAK OF OUR TRUTHS,
IT DOES NOT CONCEAL OUR WEAKNESS,
WHICH IS THAT OF OUR HEARTS.
OUR LOVE CAN'T BE DEFINED.
NOT IN ALL THE PAGES OF THIS BOOK.

FROM YOUR FAVOURITE STRANGER

I quite like the poetry. It's unique and romantic, though I still have no idea where it is coming from. One book was placed inside my panty drawer. How embarrassing to know it was opened. The second was found on my mantle. The books sit on my nightstand now, piled up against the back. At night, I read through them, trying to find clues to my mystery man.

I haven't seen Kasper since the day of bloodshed. I thought he was relentless in his attempts to seduce me, but I must have scared him off after the incident at the asylum. Maybe he isn't my stalker after all, in which case, I'm left trying to solve a question that is too complex for my withered self.

I'm exhausted. The kind of exhaustion that creeps up on you and by the time you realize just how tired you are, you don't know how to get yourself out of it.

I went to the beach once when I was a little girl. I remember swimming quite far out so I could show my father how good of a swimmer I was. But by the time I got out there, I was tired, and I didn't have anything left in me to swim back. The current kept pulling me back and I panicked. By the time my feet touched the sandy banks, I could barely move, my feet getting suctioned into the sand with each foot step. That's what I feel like now. Like I'm dragging myself to reach the shore.

I hear a knock at the door and thankfully, I'm already dressed for today. I chose a dark green pinafore that ties at the back with a white blouse underneath. My hair is in a half updo, curled and brushed out at the back, and a fresh new pair of pantyhose that I treated myself to completes my outfit.

"Beverly, how are you lovely?" I say to my neighbour that lives a few doors down. Beverly is drop dead gorgeous with blond hair she wears like Gloria Grahame.

"Hi, Ada. The girls and I were wondering if you would like to join us for Sunday brunch this week. Rosie is running it this time. Well we thought with everything going on, you could use some company. We usually get together and cook, but you don't have to join until later if you would rather not. I know with the loss of your... well, I just know how difficult these times can be."

Kind of her to offer, but I don't enjoy being pitied by the neighborhood women. Especially sweet perfect Beverly. Her story was the talk of the block for quite some time. But we all lost someone in our own way. I never was one to pry in such affairs given that we all grieve differently.

"That's very kind of you. I would love to join you, though I might not be the best company."

"Oh don't be silly. We'll change that. All you need is a good cup of tea and a few friends. We're meeting at 11:00 a.m. You know where to find us. I look forward to seeing you then."

"Thanks Bev, I'll see you then."

She turns around and as she walks away; I see a man in black turn in the opposite direction around the nearest corner. He was wearing a black coat and hat, tall it seemed, yet for a second, I could feel his eyes on me. If only I could have gotten a better look at his face without his homburg dipped down.

I hear a crash in my kitchen and run in to see my jarred peach chutney is smashed on the floor in bits. Luckily I made plenty more, but what a waste of a perfectly good jar. How on earth did it fall? I know I didn't leave it at the edge of the counter. I wouldn't be so careless with something I appreciate. I'm sure there's a perfectly logical explanation for these things. There always is.

Not long later, there's another knock on the door and I open it to see its Mr. Preston, another one of my neighbours who is a frequent visitor of Sal's.

"Mr. Preston, what brings you here today?"

"Well I came to check on you. I haven't been able to catch you lately."

Mr. Preston is a bit older, but at sixty-eight, he is still active and loving life. Whenever I catch up with him, he always has a new paper headline for us to discuss, followed by a story of his grandkids. I've always enjoyed his stories and entertain his excitement in hearing it.

"Please come in," I say, inviting him in towards my living room.

"The weather is quite nice today, isn't it? They say we're heading for some rain later on today. Maybe even a storm. Wouldn't that be fun, a good bit of thunder? Britain could use the cleanse. You know who loves a good storm, my grandson Felix. William can't stand the thunder, but Felix will wait by the window when it rains and count the time between the lightning. Funny thing he is. Just like his father really."

"I still have yet to meet your grandsons. Please bring them sometime, would you?"

"One day perhaps."

Mr. Preston sits on a chair in the corner of the room and looks around. "How have you been feeling lately with everything?"

"Well, I've been a bit down if I'm being honest. But that's only natural given the circumstances. I've been reading a lot. I find the books help."

"What kind of books?"

"Romance and poetry mostly. I just finished reading one by Thomas Hardy. Wonderful and teasing, it was called *Far From The Madding Crowd.* Have you read it?"

"I can't say I've read anything from Hardy. No, I much prefer non-fiction. A little more educational for my taste. For example, most recently I read a book about birds. Did you know a house sparrow can swim underwater during times of survival? Quite interesting birds are. And how about things around here?"

"I don't particularly like living here. Maybe one day I'll sell it and move out of the country altogether. It would be nice to travel. I always wanted to go somewhere exotic and warm."

"Yes, the cold weather here puts a damper on one's soul during the winter months, doesn't it?"

"That it does."

He looks anxious and fidgety. Standing up, he walks to the door. "Well, I best be going."

"Leaving so soon?"

"I've got another friend I have to visit. I just wanted to check in on you. Maybe I could come by for tea next week at the same time?"

"I'd love nothing more."

"Excellent. See you then, Ada."

After Mr. Preston leaves, I get to my chores of dusting, sweeping and tidying the kitchen. Before I know it, the night has fallen. I cozy up in my bed for some reading, digging into the works of E. E. Cummings as I fall asleep with my side lamp still on.

What I can only guess must be hours later, I wake to a creaky noise and notice my light is no longer on. I hear faint footsteps coming from down the hall that cause me to become highly alert from my sluggish state. I grab the knife I brought from the kitchen that I've stashed under my mattress for the past week, cover myself up with my blankets over my head like a child afraid of a monster and grip the knife handle in both hands against my chest. I'm not sure what I expect at this hour, but perhaps the spirit will think I'm asleep. I feel the bed sink down beside me and the bed sheet covering my face gets slowly pulled down.

"Shhhh," whispers a man in the dark with his finger over his lips. I react quickly, lifting the knife up to the man's throat but before it can make contact with his skin, he grabs my wrist and pushes it to the bed beside my head.

"Hello, peach."

I stare into the faint blue eyes in front of me and drop the knife.

"Have you been reading my books?"

I don't answer in my shocked state. He looks at my nightstand and see's the three books stacked and the one loosely placed next to it that I was reading tonight.

"What are you doing in my house? You can't be here," I protest.

"I thought you'd be happy to see me. I've missed you, Ada."

"You're crazy. Get —" but he puts his hand over my mouth to quiet my yell.

"Shh, sweetheart. Wouldn't want to wake the neighbours, would we? Now I'm going to remove my hand from your lips, and if you try to scream again, I'm going to replace it with my mouth. Do you understand me?"

I nod agreeingly.

"That's a good girl. My sweet angel brought me back to life. Now I'm going to bring you back."

He takes his hand and drifts it down my face, sliding it to the middle of my chest between my breasts, making his way lower as he pulls the blanket down with him.

"I'm going to need you to be nice and quiet, Ada. I want to make you feel better, you see, after all that loss. Such a terrible time you've had in this house. But I want to free you from all this. I want you to know what it's like to be reborn, to be given another chance. I'm going to need you to trust me."

"I don't understand."

"You will. You and I are fated. Now close your eyes."

I'm a silly woman and I should be screaming, fighting, running, anything but trusting this man in my home. I know three things about him; his name, his profession and his new found obsession with me, but there's a part of me stirring in curiosity that causes me to allow such trust in a stranger. Maybe he wants to kill me and if that's the reason, then I can't stop him. I'm a woman, fragile next to his form. He's strong and a doctor of all things, with the smarts to pull something like this off, no doubt. More than anything, it's the effect he has on me that I can't quite explain. The sound of his voice feels like a lullaby to my soul and maybe I've been so desperate from all these empty years that I'll take the affection given to me when offered. I close my eyes while I breathe heavily, fisting my hands tightly.

He runs his hand down my leg and gently lifts my nightgown up to my waist.

"Is this okay?" he asks.

I'm not wearing panties. I never do at night. His touch against my thighs offers me a warm sensation and I can feel my cheeks start to turn pink. "Yes," I whisper.

I feel the bed sink. My legs are spread and a wetness touches over my middle.

I take in a sharp breath at the welcomed sensation. I want more of it.

"I've longed to taste you in my nightmares, hoping for such an amnesty be given for the scenes of horror I drowned in. So many nights without you. So many nights wondering if I would ever be so lucky as to touch your skin."

He licks me again, the full length of his tongue touching every part of me, then breathes in my scent audibly.

"I've been to hell, sweetheart. This is what the heavens must feel like."

He dives back in and starts moving his tongue around in various methods until he sticks to the one I react to most. I lift my hips up and cover my mouth with my hand, trying to muffle my own moans but he can feel the vibrations of them.

"I want to hear every sound that comes out of your mouth, but tonight I want you to hear the sounds of my tongue instead and how wet you are for me."

My eyes are still closed and it wouldn't matter anyway because the room is dark. I listen to him lick me, his own breathing becoming more intense. I haven't had a proper climax in years. I'm not even sure I'm still capable of such a thing. He grips my thighs and pulls me in tighter to him with a thirsty moan from his throat, devouring me. And then I feel it peaking, the throbbing becoming all consuming. I arch my back pushing myself into him more, and grab the mattress sheet on each side of me to grip.

"Kasper," I whisper out.

He doesn't slow down and I bite my lip hard as my finish comes rolling in fiercely, my body shaking, my eyelids squeezing tight as pleasure soars through me.

When my body starts to relax, I feel his mouth pull away, giving me one last kiss on the sensitive area before leaning over my face.

"Keep your eyes closed, Ada." He places a long soft kiss on my lips. "Lick your lips."

I do as he says, noticing the flavour that remains.

"That's how you taste. Divine on my taste buds. Do you want to try more?"

"Yes," I say in my agreeable state. He brings his fingers back down below and rubs me a few times before bringing his fingers up to my lips.

"Open," he orders gently.

I do so and he slips a couple fingers inside my mouth to rub against my tongue. I feel his fingers being pulled out and then they're replaced with his mouth, his tongue hitting the same spot on my tongue that his fingers were just pressing on.

He keeps his kiss soft and light and I join in, kissing him back in the same way. His mouth moves away and I hate the way my mouth now feels empty without it.

"Do you want to see me again?" he asks.

"I – I don't know. Do I even have a choice?" I smirk.

"That's not what I asked. Ada, I'm going to ask you once more. Would you like me to visit you again?"

"Yes Kas, I'm afraid you're a puzzle I need to solve, and a bold one at that. I suppose I should give you the chance to explain yourself."

If my eyes were open, I'd bet he was smiling.

"Plenty of time for that."

The room falls to silence, leaving a stillness that I can't perceive. I feel a kiss on my forehead, the most softest, gentle kiss that takes its time.

"I knew you were in there somewhere. You'll crave every part of me soon enough. Get some sleep now. You'll need it."

He kisses my one closed eye, followed by the other. I hear footsteps follow out of my house and don't bother to open my eyes again, satisfied and so very confused. But feeling confused is better than feeling grief. It's enough for one night.

CHAPTER 9
Kasper

Damn that woman. She's going to be the end of me. The taste of her sultry nectar lingers in my memory, waiting impatiently for me to get on my knees for a chance of her essence once more.

I open up the latest of my reads, *Mental Illness of Modern Society*, turning to where I was reading on page 226, and continue studying. It seems that's all I do now when I'm not thinking about her. I've read more books in the last year than the decade before. But I need to figure out how to cure psychosis. My patients need me. Sometimes that means doing things by the book, and sometimes I merely use them for inspiration to come up with my own creative cure. After all, the research into this field is so shallow, the experiments often done without proper proof of long term results other than to numb one's mind. But I can't do that. I need answers, and I need a way to enter into an unfamiliar world.

"Doctor, I'm sorry to interrupt your train of thought. I can see you are busy, but this is important. It's regarding a patient," Nurse Arden speaks.

"Come on in," I reply.

"I know you've been working more on the second ward the last few weeks but I also know you're in the process of taking over some of Dr. Wilson's patients on the first ward. It's just that... the patient in room 111 on ward one doesn't like talking to many of the staff, but she seemed to do well with you from what I witnessed. I've convinced some of the women to invite her to their group games session, but she hasn't said a word to me since I started here and I'm wondering what you're doing differently to get her to trust you. I seem to be non-existent and I've been here for over a year. You come in with fresh eyes and you've made a breakthrough with patients that I can't quite get to. You have a gift."

Nurse Arden's attempts to inflate me feel disingenuous, but I play into it.

"If you want to be a part of her story, you need to enter her world the same as her. You can't be her nurse. You need to be her friend, or someone she can relate to in her old life."

"Hmm. Very well. Doris said you have cancelled most of her treatments. Is that wise, sir?"

"I want her mind clear. I can't fix what's inside when her brain is being manipulated in the process. It may be unconventional, but I've seen success in other cases where we work at a start from scratch approach and dig into the narrative of their psyche. It'll take time, but we'll get there."

"And what about Ms. Conners from room 120? She's been stealing again and refusing to eat. She took Miss Landry's journals the other day and today Nurse Reba said her chart notes from another patient were found under her bedding. She's scheduled for a hydrotherapy session at 11:00 but you may want to address this."

"Let's cut her session time in half. I'll take care of it after."

"Very well. Thank you Doctor... for your advice. You're so very good at your job. The patients seem to love you. The staff as well." She smiles coyly as pink flows up into her cheeks.

Nurse Arden is a beautiful woman. Colleen is her first name. I looked into all of the staff when I first got here. She's a young twenty-four year old with a set of brown eyes as dark as chocolate and long black hair with a tanned complexion. Taller than the average woman, she has long legs and a full chest that I'm sure any man would be grateful to explore. But to be honest, I've always been more of a butt guy, and now that I have Ada, I can't picture being with anyone but her. Colleen looks like a temptation that would have worked on me years ago, but now I see her as nothing more than a young nurse trying to test the waters, and it sure as hell won't be with me.

"Anything else, Nurse?" I ask, trying to avert my eyes from her and back to my book.

She hesitates for a moment before shaking her head. In return, I nod mine toward the door and she leaves, closing it on her way out.

CHAPTER 10

Kasper

By the time I get home from my shift, it's nearly 8:00 p.m. The day never ends when it's supposed to, courtesy of Mrs. Bennett from room 101 who decided she would run through the halls naked once again, declaring to the world that beings from the sea were coming.

When I walk into my place, it's eerily quiet, unlike the normal noise from the neighboring flats I usually hear. I set down my suitcase that's filled with mostly books and a bit of paperwork for me to look into regarding some new patients that are set to arrive this week.

The first thing I notice is my window is slightly ajar. I don't normally keep it open when I'm gone, even in the summer heat. I don't trust any of these tenants to not get nosey while I'm away. But there it is, open just a couple inches. I'm second guessing myself, wondering if I did happen to leave it open. Nothing else looks amiss in my place until I walk into my bedroom and notice a small piece of paper sticking out from my nightstand drawer. It's only the corner of a paper and when I open my drawer, I see it's just the work contract I signed when I started at the asylum. I put all my paperwork in that drawer, and I haven't had any need to go through anything in it for quite some time. The papers are unorganized and definitely not how I left them and then I start to panic. Someone was in here.

I shuffle through the pile of papers and don't see anything missing from it. It's all here. But that doesn't make me feel any better because the contents of this drawer are confidential as any paperwork belonging to someone should be. I get on my knees and gently pull open the hidden compartment on the bottom of the nightstand. It's where I keep my most important documents, my birth certificate and everything about my life before the war. Everything is just as it was, and I breathe a sigh of relief that whoever came into this place didn't find that drawer. The last thing I need is for my plan to be spoiled before I make real progress.

I continue to look around, going through each drawer, checking to make sure nothing has been taken. Mind you, I don't have much. Not even a small television. I have no need for one when books occupy most of my time, and when the books don't, the stories I make up of Ada do.

I've gone easy on her. I've tried to be understanding of her situation, empathetic even, if I can even muster such an emotion nowadays. But for her, I try. However, my little damsel in distress is in need of a wake up. She needs to understand her new reality will be with me. Her past won't have to haunt her anymore once I'm in it. Hell, I already am. I'm her cure, her way to break herself out of this spell of grief she's been feeling. Before she knows it, she will be begging me to make me hers. What she doesn't know is that she already is.

Knock Knock Knock. "Dr. Knight!" I hear from my door.

I walk over to it and open it up knowing the familiarity of the voice behind it.

"Hi Ms. Turner. How can I help you on this fine evening," I reply as my landlady stands with blushed cheeks in her house dress. She lives on the main floor, a spinster who owns this property due to the inheritance from her own father who passed before the war. Miss

Molly Turner is in her mid fifties, and convincing her to lease me this flat was as easy as offering her a slice of cake. A little flirting and some fresh flowers cut from the park was all it took to convince her that Dr. Knight needed a place to stay to take care of his very vulnerable patients. She's a rounded woman and always wears her greying hair up high in a 1910's style she has yet to retire. Her clothes hardly match the time either, still remaining quite conservative despite her forward personality, a complete contrariety in itself.

"Well, Dr. Knight, I was just stopping by because I had some extra cottage pie from dinner and I thought perhaps you might be hungry after your long shift. It's such good work you do helping all those feeble minded patients of yours."

"How kind of you Ms. Turner. I am quite hungry actually. You wouldn't believe the kinds of things I had to deal with today."

"Oh, I've only heard stories myself. James Montgomery, do you know the name? He was the son of Phillip Montgomery. They were big landowners. A handsome young chap. Used to see him at the church festivals on occasion. His parents were big supporters. Anyway, James went to war and came back with strange paranoia. Shot his own father with a gun in the middle of the night. His father was alright, thankfully. Only a flesh wound, but they put him in Northfield after that. Such a shame really. He had so much potential."

I don't have much to add to her story. That could have been me. So I politely take the dish from her hand. "This looks delicious. I'll be sure to drop the dish off to you later. Cheers."

She nods and begins to turn away but then stops herself. "Oh I meant to tell you, there was someone that stopped by earlier that tried to get into the building. He said he was looking for an old friend and then described what you looked like, but when I mentioned the only man that fit that description was Dr. Knight, he told me he must have been mistaken. Seemed like a nice enough bloke but not in the same class as you, of course. I got rid of him, anyway."

I don't have any friends or anyone looking for me, so her statement throws me off.

"What did he look like?" I inquire.

"Well, he was a bit shorter than you, but not by much. His hair was dark, the same as his eyes, and he had a scar across his cheek. Quite a large one too."

The description doesn't ring a bell and I'm going through the backlog of encounters in my head of the possibilities of my visitor. Could he have been the one snooping through my flat?

"Well I'm sure it was just a misunderstanding. Thank you for handling that Miss. Turner," I reply.

She waves her hand back as she walks away.

I re-enter my flat, placing the cottage pie down on the small two seater table, scratching my head to figure out my mystery friend.

I've always kept a low profile. Not for any reason other than I didn't care to connect with people. Everyone feels like a fraud in this world, and I'm no different. We all wake up and put on our best face to enter a society where we have to pretend we are somebody. If there is one thing I've learned from the war, it's that we're just another number, and those people we once called friends end up dead, putrefying in the ground while we move on without them until we face our own end. There's only one connection I care about now, and it's the one that will live on long past our deaths. I can separate myself from the rest of existence but not her.

CHAPTER 11

Ada

I never know what to wear to these things. I stand in the mirror flattening my dress down with my palm as I stare at my reflection, the paleness in my face coming through more with the red of this dress. I should change, put on something more suitable for my skin tone perhaps, but I don't have the energy today to care. I add a little rouge to my cheeks to brighten my complexion and some soft pink lipstick. I hate wearing lipstick, always wondering if it's trailed its way to my teeth, which is why I've always gone for the lighter shades. Adding just a touch of colour to my lips gives the illusion of fullness. My bottom lip is more plump than my upper lip, unlike Kasper's, who are equally sized to perfection. I've never wanted a pair of lips on me like I've wanted his. I am not this person, yearning for the touch of a man, but I can't seem to get our last encounter out of my head.

I check my wrist watch and notice the time. I'm already running a few minutes late. By the time I get there, I realize I forgot the potato salad I made in the fridge. How silly of me. Rosie insists it's no big deal and there is plenty of food to go around, but I still can't help feeling the rush of guilt that sweeps over me.

Beverly calls me over to sit with her and another woman named Silvia that she has introduced me to. Silvia is tall, very tall, with copper red hair and masculine features with a bold set of cheek bones that stand out.

"We were just discussing the old rumours of this place. Did you know in this very room, someone was murdered?" Silvia says.

"Now now," Beverly intervenes. "Don't scare the little thing. She's finally made it out to a luncheon and you're going to start with that?"

"Oh please, don't hold back on my account. I love a good story. Go on," I insist.

Silvia continues. "Well, you see this land used to be used as a burial ground of sorts, or so that's what I've been told. Now I don't know the entire story, but I do know that there was a woman who used to live here and it was said that she was visited by the spirits of the dead. Apparently it drove her crazy, so much that one night, she snuck out of her room after hearing voices, came into this very space and collapsed. They found her the next day, blue in the face with not a single wound on her. Some say she had a heart attack, some say she took pills, but they never found anything in her, you see. I don't think she took her own life. I think it was the ghosts that killed her."

"Can they do that, ghosts killing people?" Beverly asks.

"Sure they can. They must be able to. At least the ones sent by the devil," Silvia explains.

"And Rosie's okay with living here, knowing that she lives on the grounds of a burial and that a woman died in her home in this very living room?" I whisper, being aware that Rosie's not far from hearing.

Beverly and Silvia look at each other for a moment, as if an unspoken conversation is going on between them.

Silvia speaks first, reluctantly so, "We all live over the dead, my dear. We all have ghosts following us."

Rosie interjects just then. "Please, go help yourselves to some food. There's plenty to go around for everyone."

It's the break we needed to lighten the mood. We each fill our plates. I place a couple finger sandwiches on mine, with a scone and some jam as well as some sort of salad with pear that looks interesting. I pour myself a cup of tea and head back to the small table set up where Beverly and Silvia were first sitting. It's not a large space by any means, but enough for a few small tables and chairs, lined with lace tablecloth.

I look over to see Rosie and Silvia talking amongst themselves, looking over in my direction for a glance, almost as in gossip. I've always felt like an outcast wherever I go. Perhaps that's why I prefer to avoid these types of events. Beverly has always been so kind to me, but the rest of these women judge me, the same as I was judged by Edward's family and friends. I just don't belong here.

Another woman sits down beside me, placing her plate down next to mine.

"I'm Jolene. I think I've seen you around here before, but who knows. There's always so many new faces here I can hardly keep up. It's a nice thing, to be able to all get together like this, more so without the men. Trouble, they are. Do you have a man back home?"

Jolene is the opposite of Silvia. She is short and more plump, especially around the face. Her plate is twice as full as mine. Her hair is greying in certain spots amongst her dusty light brown hair and she wears little makeup with just a simple cream day dress. She has a tweak of a Welsh accent to her, and I wonder how she of all people ended up knowing Rosie, who was always quite picky with who she associated herself with.

"I –" I pause for a second not knowing quite how to respond. I don't have a man anymore. Do I tell her I'm a widow? The last thing I want is someone asking questions about my past. So I decide to answer with as little information as possible.

"I'm seeing someone but it's not serious. Do you?" There is truth in my words, though not the whole truth and I hope she cares more to talk about her own situation than ask about mine.

"Nah, men are nothing but trouble. It's the only reason I'm here today, to get away from all the nonsense. Only one good thing that comes from men, and half of them don't know what they're doing to give it to ya, if you know what I mean. They are like cockroaches. You can squish them under your feet all ya want, and they still come back from the dead for more. Can't get rid of them buggers."

"Surely they aren't all like that. Maybe you've just had some bad luck," I reply.

"You have yet to see the worst of them if you still believe that. Tell me, how long have you known your mister?"

"Not long. It's new."

"Well there ya have it. Just you wait. They are all the same in the end. You'll see."

Beverly sits down beside us. "I see you've met Mrs. Bevan."

She interjects, "You know not to call me that. Jolene is the only name I'll listen to. Bevan is a curse, one I wish to be rid of.

"I thought you didn't have a man? *Mrs?*" I ask.

"That's not here nor there. Excuse me," Jolene says, getting up and walking to the desserts to add more to her plate.

"Don't mind her," Beverly explains. "She doesn't like to talk about it. Her husband and her have a dark history. It's probably not my story to tell, but she's a loyal friend to the women here. She may be very frank, but she means well."

I nod in understanding.

"You've lived here for quite some time and yet are still so unfamiliar with us. Why don't you visit with us more often?" Beverly asks.

"I just prefer to be alone, I guess. Please don't take offense to that. I keep busy with my job and my hobbies."

"You should think about coming around more often. You're not far off, only a short walk away."

"Thank you. If I can pry my eyes away from my books long enough, then perhaps," I joke.

I don't overstay my welcome and leave shortly after I'm done with my second helping of tea.

I get back with plenty of time left to the day, deciding to change out of this red dress into something a little more casual. I step into a comfortable cotton day dress, a plaid blue one with a black collar around the neck line, and walk to my bed, stunned to see yet another book.

This one is familiar: *Pride and Prejudice* by Jane Austen. I know I've seen this book before. I flip through it, trying to remember if I have indeed read this one in my previous days.

There's a handwritten poem on the inside with the same recognizable handwriting, the same as there has been with all the others.

My Elizabeth
Our story we will weave into every fibre of cloth
That warms our flesh
Mended by the mischief of our unity
Our fortress sealed within our hearts
And in these circumstances
In which we believe we are to be

As tulip bulbs hide in the winters soil
Until it is time

From your* knight *in shining armour

Time for what, I question. I feel as though these poems are clues to something bigger, and though I feel awakened by it, I'm also questioning why it makes me uncomfortable. Not in the way that one feels unsafe about something. Not even in the way one dreads such confrontation, but in the familiar way one loses something before they can even get a chance to hold onto it.

Grief comes in waves, like peeling off each layer of an onion, waiting to see which triggers my tears. I don't wish to face loss again, and I think the fear of that prevents me from being able to absorb the adoration that I'm offered. But Kasper triggers something in me that makes me feel greedy for it. I barely know the man really and truly, and yet there is a familiarity in his presence that I know without knowing. Perhaps that's similar to our faith, believing in something that has yet to show itself in its fullness.

I hear another noise, footsteps walking away from the hall. I run to catch them red handed, but when I enter the hall, there is no one there. My bedroom door slams behind me. A drift perhaps, or something more.

CHAPTER 12

Kasper

Ada's restless tonight, her needs of sleep ignored. She's getting ready to spend the next hour setting her hair despite the fact that it's 2:00 a.m. But tonight, I want her hair down, to run my fingers through the damp strands of her freshly washed hair. She doesn't see me yet, standing beside her wardrobe. The night is quiet, the only rumblings come from the outside street.

She's wearing a pink silk robe that shows the peaks of her nipples, and I can't help but think of how good they would taste in my mouth. She sits down at her vanity, the mirror slightly broken in the top corner, the wood frame around it worn and chipped. She brushes her soft hair, holding the golden handle in her hands so delicately, and when I step out from beside her wardrobe, her eyes lock with mine in the mirror. She doesn't speak, frozen with the brush now unmoving, gripping it tighter at my appearance.

"Hello, peach," I say.

I move closer to her, remove the brush from her hand and start to run it over her dark auburn strands. She drops her hands onto her lap, still eyeing me ever so carefully through the mirror, our eyes unmoving while I continue to gently brush her hair.

"How did you get in here?" she asks.

"The same way as I always do. How did you get in here?" I repeat her question, this time pointing the brush to my heart. I place the brush down on the vanity and sweep her hair away from her neck, a lightness to my touch causing a shiver down her spine.

She turns around to me, our faces within inches of each other but instead, pushes me away. I stand fully and she follows. I can't help but draw my eyes down her body, that silk robe being the only thing that is standing in the way of me being able to worship her flesh.

"Kas, you can't be here. I –"

"You what? Do you really want me to leave, Ada?" I ask, approaching her once more. "Say the words and I'll leave right now."

Her lips part slightly and her chest moves up and down more rapidly. I pull on the rope of her robe, tugging her against my body. She gasps at the sudden move.

"Don't you see how you long for me? There's a fire in you that burns. I can feel your heat. I found you despite everything. I found you," I repeat.

Her eyes soften and stare at my lips and her cheeks deepen their hue of pink. "Kasper, this is crazy. I barely know you. And yet I can't think of another reason to stop this."

"Baby, we don't need to follow the rules. We can do things our way."

"No, Kasper. I can't. We can't!"

She paces the room for a minute before walking over to the window to stare out at the night sky. I come up behind her and move the hair away from her shoulder and lay one single kiss on her skin. She exhales in relief at the contact of my lips.

"I know you, Ada. I know you in all your moods. I know you in all your fantasies. I know what you dream about. And I know what you fear. You don't fear me."

"I suppose I don't, but in my dreams you get to be who I want you to be."

"And who do you want me to be?" I ask.

"Everything."

She turns around from the window to face me and looks at me so vulnerably. I just want to wrap her in my arms and never let her go.

"You've hypnotized me, you see. I can't see straight anymore. But I want to walk this crooked path with you. I need to tell you something, Ada, and if after I've told you it, you want me to leave, I will. But if you want, I'll stay. And if you ask me to stay, then I'm going to take all of you and never let you go free from my hold. But I won't do this dishonestly."

I reach into my back trouser pocket and grab my wallet, pulling out the old photo of her and hand it to her.

She places her hand over her mouth and takes a step back against the window, her gaze unwavering on the photo.

"How did you–?"

"Fate. Your late husband was my bed mate for a bit. I was there when he died. I didn't know him well, but he talked about you. The nurse gave me this picture, thinking it was mine. It wasn't, but it kept me alive all these years. I'm sorry you lost your husband. And I'm not. He couldn't help you. He didn't know how to talk to you even though he loved you. But I know what you need. I understand death the same as you. I've seen it. I've felt it. I've embraced it, begged for it even. But you make me want to live and I want to do the same for you."

"I don't understand what's happening? Why are we here?" She looks around the room, confusion panning on her face. She's about to break.

"Ada, look at me." She's shaking now, her breath staggered. "I need you to look at me." I hold her upper arms, squeezing them gently.

"I'll be your everything. I love you. Do you hear me? I love you for more reasons than make sense. I love you without understanding the origins. I love you without knowing the destination. I love you without any expectation, without any hesitancy because you and I are destined. It doesn't have to make sense to anyone else but us. I know you feel it. I know you want to believe it. I'm not asking for the words back. I'm just asking you to venture into this life with me, bit by bit, step by step and maybe one day, you'll feel it. Maybe one day, you'll love me too."

She presses her hand against my chest, against one of the scars that lays underneath my shirt, looking into my watery eyes. I'm trying to hold back my manhood from escaping from them, but a part of me doesn't care. A part of me wants to break too.

"I don't understand love. I don't know how to feel it anymore. I think I've lost it too many times. But I feel something and I don't want for that to go away. I don't want for you to go away," Ada says, her lips moving up to meet mine.

She breaks our kiss but I pull her back into me, continuing the passion we had sparked before. I reach down to her waist and release her robe tie, the silk parting at the middle. I move my hands to the top of her shoulders and push the fabric back to fall off of her body, leaving her bare in front of me. She doesn't protest; instead, she presses herself into me more, feeling the heat between us, my hardness pressing into her stomach.

"Do you want to be my angel?"

She nods in quiet desperation.

I smile in response. Of course she does. She wants to submit, to let go of control. She just doesn't know how. She's constantly wound up, trying to hold onto whatever grasp of her old reality that keeps her thinking she's sane, but she's the furthest thing from it and I want to lose all lucidity with her, to fall head first into her world just so she doesn't have to be alone in it.

"Get on your knees and show me your halo."

She furrows her brow slightly, almost if second guessing, but does as she's told, looking up at me with those honey irises of hers. I take my white button down shirt off first, letting her see the scars that have branded me. I undo my trouser button and pull down the zipper, dropping both my pants and my white under shorts to my ankles to reveal myself to her. I'm as hard as hard gets but with Ada, it's causing an uncomfortable throbbing inside of more than just my cock.

"Have you been thinking about this?" I ask.

She just stares with a mouth watering gaze, her eyes wide at what's in front of her.

I step out of my pants all together. It's only fair that I should be as vulnerable with her as she is for me.

She eyes my scars along my chest, bringing the tips of her fingers to run along them. She stands up to get closer to them, walking around the back of me to see the continuation of them on my backside. They are worse on my chest, but she takes it all in, every single one, seeing the damage left on the vessel that I live inside. She gets back to the front of me, the look of concern imprinted on her face and lowers herself to me once more.

"I *have* been thinking about this," she finally speaks. "Every spare moment of my day, I think of you sneaking into my house and what it would be like to see you, to feel you, to taste you."

She wraps her hand around my cock, feeling and exploring what's hers, then gently licks. I moan in response. She uses her tongue to wet every part of my length until she moves into rhythm, her head moving in and out of me while she uses her hand to grip at the base with a perfect pressure. Staring down at her taking me in is a vision I have only dreamed of while distracting myself from the nightmares that used to eat me alive, and now, my sweet angel is pleasuring me with a look on her face that says it's equally as pleasurable for her.

"That's it. You're doing it perfectly," I say, the praise eliciting a moan from her.

My God, this woman is going to have my legs shaking in no time. "Stop," I implore her.

She does so but looks up at me confused. "Is it not to your liking?"

"On the contrary, love. It's too good. Stand up."

She does as I ask and I don't give her a second more before my lips are pressed up against her fervently, my tongue exploring her mouth, my body heat radiating against her. She wraps her arms around the back of my neck while I pull her waist into me tighter.

"I want you, Kasper. I haven't done this in a long time and I'm nervous but I think I need you."

"Yes, baby. You do. Just as much as I need you."

I lift her up, cradled in my arms and place her gently on her bed, taking a second longer to stare down at her nakedness, how sleek her skin looks against the accent of the moon light coming in from the window.

I move in between her legs, hovering over her body in anticipation.

"I'm gonna take you now, Ada, and then you're really mine. There will be no escaping me. I won't leave you for all the money or pleasures in the world. Is this what you want, baby? For me to chase you to the ends of the earth? To never let you breathe air that is not shared with me? To never let another man touch you ever again? This is your only warning, peach. Is this what you really want?"

She runs her hand through my hair, gripping it at the back, pulling my head down towards her face.

"I want this. I need you. I don't know why yet, but I do."

I smile wickedly at her, knowing she'll forever be my undoing. I place the head of my cock against her entrance and wait for her impatience to grow. She lifts up her hips to me and pulls my back closer into her body. I slowly enter her, letting her adjust to my size, knowing it's been a while since she's been intimate with anyone. She's coated in her own wetness, ready for me in more ways than I could have envisioned. It's a feeling unlike anything I've ever experienced, this moment of unity. I push in, feeling her walls clench against me and we both moan into each other's mouths. It feels as though our world has simultaneously collapsed around us and exploded at the same time. Her breathing intensifies as I thrust in and out of her, keeping it teasingly slow.

"Kas," she says in a whisper. Hearing my name come out of her mouth with such yearning is pulling at the strings of my heart.

"Baby, you make me insane," I say back to her, grabbing her breast in my hand while kissing along her neck. I twist her nipple in my fingers, adding some pressure and intensity to the sensations running through her. She responds greedily, arching her back further into me and tilting her head to the side to expose more of her skin to my lips. I drag my tongue back up to her mouth and bite down on that precious bottom lip of hers. She releases another moan, but I silence it with my mouth as I start to quicken the pace of my thrusts below.

She's pushing her hips into me while I'm feeding her my cock with more intensity. This woman is insatiable. I'm practically melting into her with how strong my need is for her closeness.

"I think I... Oh God, Kasper I can't–" she says, right before her body ignites, the evidence of her pleasure escaping in the muted cries from her mouth. Her head tilts back, her eyes close and her body shakes as her orgasm forces through her.

I can feel her contract around me and it spins me into my own finishing, pulsating inside her as I experience the most intense feeling of my life. We're both breathless, finding each other again as the earth settles, staring into her eyes in a moment I can only describe as euphoric. If heaven is anything less than this, I don't want it. I just want her in whatever form we become as long as it's together.

I rest my forehead against hers as we both close our eyes. All the previous tension between us dissipates, and I roll on my back beside her, barely enough room for us on the small mattress.

She turns towards me, placing her hand on my chest and her leg over mine.

"That was wonderful, Kasper. I think it was more than wonderful."

I smile at her in awe of her beauty but more so of her surrender.

"I want to see more of you. I like this feeling. It's been so long. I just... I can't lose it again. It's too hard. Can you promise me that? That you're not going to leave me? I can't bear the thought of it. It's been so lonely. I think it'll ruin me if you abandon me. If you can't promise me it, if God himself can't promise me it, then I can't do this again."

"I'll bargain with the devil if I have to," I reply, trying to ease her mind. "I promise."

She breathes a sigh of relief, or something else I can't quite figure out. Her eyes are roaming as if they are taking in new information.

"Can I see you tomorrow?" she asks. "I'm having a visit with Mr. Preston, an old friend but I'd like to see you after."

"Sure, I'll come by when I'm done work."

"I'll leave the door unlocked for you." She curls up closer to me, closing her eyes.

I whisper back, "You always do."

CHAPTER 13

Ada

Like a fever dream, I see the flashbacks of my mother. She's standing in the corner of my bedroom, a shadow of a person, with her long black hair and her evil grin. I know what she wants, what she always wanted. It's every part of my happiness that she can take for herself.

"You can't have him, Ada," she says.

I know I'm sleeping but I feel like I can interact all the same.

Demon, I hear a whisper from behind me in a deep voice, even though she's still standing in front of me. But then who's behind me?

"He's not yours for the taking," she says, swaying in the corner of the darkness.

"He loves me," I say.

She laughs in response, a laugh so vile, black tar oozes from between her teeth and seeps down her chin. "He doesn't love you. How could anyone love you? You really are so delusional. It's no wonder your mother tried to kill you."

"I don't have a mother anymore," I correct her.

She looks just like my mother though, only possessed and covered in the markings of evil.

Get her. The voice behind me whispers. A chill runs through me and the shadow tilts its head at me.

"You aren't supposed to be here. Get out of my room."

She laughs again. "You're not good enough for him. You'll never be good enough for him. You're just an experiment and once he's done with you, he'll throw you away and find someone who still has their mind."

"GET OUT!" I yell.

She doesn't budge, just keeps laughing incessantly. I run towards her and wrap my hands around her neck. My fingers grip into the leather of her skin and I refuse to lessen my grip when I see the surprise on her face. I can do whatever I want in my own dream, and I want this demon gone.

Don't let up, the voice says. I'm putting every ounce of my energy into killing the creature in front of me once and for all. She grabs my arms, trying to rip them away from her throat, but I don't falter. I'm giving her what she deserves, her own suffering.

"Ada!" I hear my name. "Ada! Look at me!"

I stop for a brief second. I'm waking up. My dream is over. The shadow in front of me disappears and Kasper is standing in front of me.

"Ada, you had a bad dream. Are you okay?" I'm confused. So very confused.

"It was a dream." I repeat. "It was a dream. Sometimes I sleepwalk, I think."

"That's okay. Let's get you back to bed, okay?"

"Okay," I agree. "I'm sorry, I didn't mean to wake you. Is it morning? Did you stay all night?"

"I slipped out to the kitchen to make you some breakfast and heard you yelling."

I rub my head. I haven't had a dream like that in a while. How strange.

"I think maybe I just need to get some fresh air today. I think that would help."

"I'm going to finish up your breakfast, but I'll be back, okay?"

I nod, getting back under the covers. He kisses me on the forehead and leaves the room, and it feels empty in here, too empty.

Last night was incredible. I haven't felt something so powerful in all my life. I have feelings for a man I barely know. Yet our souls feel like they've known each other for our entire existence. The story of Kasper is unveiling itself slowly to me. The man tracked me down with little knowledge of me from my deceased husband and a bloodied picture, and yet the lengths he went to for me don't go unnoticed. In normal circumstances, a woman might report him to the authorities. But I crave love as much as I fear it. I crave the obsession of it and the rush of it. I love feeling wanted and worshiped. Perhaps it derives from my own mothers neglect, but to know that there is someone in the world that sees me, really sees me in all my flaws and still desires me wholeheartedly, well I don't think there is anything quite like that to live for.

Kasper returns with my food but none for him.

"Are you not hungry?" I ask.

"I'm not really one for eating breakfast."

"Oh. I suppose there's a lot that I don't yet know."

"Yet," he emphasizes and winks.

"Tell me about your family."

"My family?" He sighs. "It's complicated."

I can see him shifting uncomfortably. Maybe I'm opening old wounds but nonetheless, I know so little that I need to try and pry any information out of him that he'll give me, so I urge him on.

"I can handle complicated."

"Well, my father died in the first war. My mother shortly after of the Spanish flu. I was sent to live with a distant aunt, and I suppose I was happy there for a bit. She had a son named Thomas. He and I were only a year apart. We got along well. But he died after about a year of my stay. We had wandered into town one day to run a couple of errands for my aunt and he was hit by a car. My aunt blamed me. Her own husband had disappeared years before, so it was just us. I lived with her until I turned sixteen and then she too passed away from pneumonia. We were both very sick that year but I made it and she didn't. I felt like I cursed everyone with my presence, the child who brought death upon whoever he touched. So after that I was on my own and I tried to stay that way, not letting myself get close to anyone. I worked my way up, learning different skills until I was offered a good steady position at the —"

He pauses for a second.

"Bethlam?" I fill in.

"Well, not quite. It's more complicated than that with education and such, but I got here eventually."

"Well, to have made it so far under such harsh circumstances. That's pretty admirable. Not everyone can make something out of their life that has been through so much suffering, so much loss."

"I had a pretty good motivation after the war," he smiles crookedly.

I lean in for a brief kiss, but before I can pull away he deepens our kiss for a second longer.

I hear a knock at the door and he swiftly gets up.

"Do you mind?" he asks me.

"No, please. I'm not even dressed yet."

He walks to the door and I hear him explain to my visitor that we'll need some time to get ready yet.

"Just the old friend you were mentioning that you were visiting with. I told him to come back in an hour."

"Oh right, Mr. Preston. He's early. Well thank you for the food. I should get dressed. Thank you for ... everything."

"I'll see you soon. I've gotta get ready for work myself, so."

"Of course."

I close the door behind him and head back to start my day with a little bit more sunshine to light the day ahead. His scent of bergamot and coffee lingers, encapsulating his presence despite his departure. There's something about his energy that feels different today, and I can't quite put my finger on it. I know he's holding back on something. I want to pry everything out of his head and absorb it into my own but I suppose a little patience will help me solve the riddle of Kasper Knight.

CHAPTER 14

Kasper

This morning has not gotten off to a great start. I wish I could tell Ada my truth, but I know it will change everything and I'm not ready for what's to come just yet. I have things to prepare but I'm starting to feel this urgency or perhaps a restlessness of sorts. More than anything, I don't want to start our relationship off with lies and yet there's a large part of my identity that I've had to keep from her for her own safety. I would like to think I'm in this grey area of doing it for the right reasons, but I know the rest of the world won't see it that way. They'll claim it was the devil on my shoulder and I'll claim it as love. If it ends in their favour, I'll be denied the one thing I can't live without, and so my cautiousness is vital.

Dr. Wilson has called me into his office to discuss patient 111, one of the cases he mentioned he would be assigning to me upon my hiring as he gradually lightened his patient load. It is wreaking the kind of havoc in my life that has my head spinning in too many directions, making me nauseous.

"What happened this morning?" Dr. Wilson asks me, looking down on me suspiciously.

"I can't say that I could tell you. The patient was hysterical. I was off duty but got there as I arrived for my shift."

"She tried to kill me!" Nurse Arden exclaims. "This is the job I chose, but that woman is dangerous. The patient needs to be transferred to a proper facility."

"It's likely she will have some residual effects with the change in the routine of her care, including the elimination of her insulin therapy," I try to explain. "Temporary, I assure you. This case is a hard one, but I have all the confidence that we're almost there. In the meantime, I think it would be wise to move Nurse Arden to the other ward, just to give things time to cool down."

"Though I don't agree with you stopping her insulin therapy, I think you're right in saying that it would be wise to move Nurse Arden. Not only for her safety, but the safety of the patient," Dr. Wilson agrees. "But don't get your hopes up. These episodes of psychosis can last weeks with her. Just when we think we make progress, she reverts into that state. It's one of the hardest cases I've seen with her condition. I've seen some recover from it, but I've seen too many more lose their minds for good."

Nurse Arden protests the change. "Moving me is not necessary. There are of course some patients that have been proving to be more difficult, but I can handle this. I'm not sure why she hates me so much. I took your advice, Dr. Knight. She's a vile woman. I don't know if anyone can help her. At least not here."

"Nurse, you'll be transferred to the second ward for the week. You can switch with Nurse Walden in the meantime. I'll make the arrangements. You can go now."

"Yes, sir." She exits, looking back at me for a moment longer, a look on her face I can't quite discern. Perhaps part seduction and part mischief.

"If you could close the door, Knight. I'd like to talk to you for a second."

He always calls me Knight rather than Doctor. It annoys me to no end, likely his way of holding authority over me, but I let it slide because this job is everything to me.

I have a question for you. You said you went to Cambridge University, isn't that right?"

"Yes, that's correct."

He contemplates his next question for a moment, not removing his eyes from mine.

"It's the funniest thing because you see, I bumped into an old colleague the other day who used to work at Bethlem. You said you started there for your initial year, isn't that right?"

Fuck.

"Yes, that's right. It was for a short time, mainly as a learning role. I was working under Dr. Frederick Carson during that first year."

"It seems Dr. Carson passed away just before the war. Did you know that?"

"I did not." *Of course I did.*

"It was cancer of the lungs, I was told. Tell me, do you remember a man named Frank Berns? He was a running board member at the time. Oversaw all the hiring."

"I don't think that name is familiar," I reply with unease.

"Well, he seems to remember you. He said Winston Knight showed great prospects in his first year and was wondering how you were doing here all these years later."

"I'm sorry, I can't put a face to the name. It's been so long. With the war and all, most of my memories before then are a blur."

"Right. You were sent over to France in attempts to help the young men experiencing war neurosis. Which base were you stationed at again?"

"I was at uhhh… " I'm catching myself trying to figure out how to not raise any further suspicions. "It was 117, until I was transferred. And well, as you know, I didn't make it to the next."

"Hmmm." He taps his hand against his leg. "Very well. You may go."

I nod and leave, my heart beating out of my fucking chest. I can't blow this. If I do, it will ruin every damn thing I've worked up to until this point.

I leave his office and Nurse Arden is waiting outside the door.

"I think we're done here, Nurse. You heard what he said. Second ward."

"I was hoping to talk to you privately if you have a minute before I head over."

"I don't, actually. I have patients to check up on."

"This won't take long. I must insist."

"Very well," I reply. I follow her down the corridor to the rec room that is currently empty. A group meeting will begin in here shortly but for now, the space is vacant. Nurse Arden shuts the door behind us.

"You had a visitor stop by last night. I assumed you had gone home by then. He said it was urgent, that he needed to talk to you, but wouldn't leave his name. Said he was an old friend. Here," she picks a piece of paper out of her pocket and hands it to me. On it is the address of a nearby hotel with his room number.

"Thank you. I'll take care of this. Oh uh… what did he look like?"

"Dark features, scar over his face. Very quiet demeanor."

I nod, still puzzled with who this could be. First my apartment, now my work.

Nurse Arden flattens her hand on my chest and leans in close. "You know doctor, I can keep secrets too." She tries to brush her lips to my cheek and I turn her around and pin her against the door by her shoulders.

"Careful, Nurse. I don't play games."

She smiles, "Oh, but I think you do."

I step back enough to let her free and she walks away with a smug grin on her face that I want to smack off.

Lunch hour soon approaches and I don't wait any longer to find out who's been trying to track me. I drive downtown to where the red sign hangs, the old Rutherford Hotel still standing even after all these years. The R is slightly tilted down, as if it was knocked off its original stance.

I don't wait to be greeted once I'm in. I head to the 4th floor of the old building, taking the stairs up. By the time I get to the top, I take a minute to catch my breath, rubbing my palm on my back where the ache is starting to act up.

Room 408 has an occupied sign on the door knob but I don't let that deter me.

I knock three times, light enough to only hopefully catch the attention of the man inside this room. I can sense someone standing on the other side of the green wooden door, likely looking at me through the peephole.

The chain lock releases and the door opens. I stare for a second longer at the man in front of me.

"Jimmy Baker. Why, I'll be."

"Hello Dr. Knight. I believe you and I have some catching up to do."

Fuck fuck fuck!

He welcomes me into his room, motioning for us to sit down at two small chairs at the back of the room by the window. The wallpaper on the walls is peeling and the carpet smells musty. The bedspread is a floral pattern that looks worn out, no different than the rest of this place.

"What brings you to town?" I ask

"I could ask you the same thing. I thought you were dead. And then one day, I'm in town for an appointment with a new doctor. I get these wicked headaches you see, and this doctor was supposed to be the best. And who's walking in front of me on my way out? I could have sworn it was the ghost of Jude Bailey, but I wasn't entirely sure with you ahead of me so I followed you. When I saw you go into your building, you turned your head back just long enough for me to see that it was indeed you."

I had gone for a walk that day to clear my head and visit the local bookshop only a few blocks away from my place, but I knew I had eyes on me. I just didn't know they were Jimmy's. I stay silent trying to figure out Jimmy's intentions with his new information.

"How long are you planning on playing that role for, because you and I both know you are no doctor. Don't get me wrong, I'd never doubt your intelligence, but your lack of privilege speaks for itself. From cleaning floors to curing patients. I'll give credit where credit is due. You fooled a lot of people. Even your landlady sings your praises. So how'd you do it?"

"Carefully. It's complicated."

"Let me guess. To win over some sweetheart? Maybe a woman with a good family and some money? Impress her enough to fall for you? No woman with class would date a man who runs the maintenance of a building. So you take matters into your own hands. You always did like the idea of your own authority, even in the military, working up in the ranks."

Jimmy was a friend I made when our units came together towards the end of 1943. We fought side by side, telling each other about our lives, knowing we were in our final days. I never thought I'd see him again.

"I saw you get shot only fifty feet away from me. I tried to get to you but they pulled me back. You were shot," I tell him.

He moves the neck of his shirt to the side to show me a bullet wound just above his heart. "Got me good, but not enough to take me down. I heard you had a bloody building fall on you. How the hell did you survive that?"

"I'm still wondering that myself."

"It's good to see you, man."

"Yea you too." I push my fist lightly into the area by his bullet scar, shaking my head at him.

"So tell me about her," he insists.

I grab the picture that I keep on me at all times, worn out after all these years, handing it to him.

"She's a pretty one. You going to marry her?"

"Yea, I am. She doesn't exactly know the truth, and I would appreciate it if you could keep your silence regarding my position."

"You're going to have to tell her sooner or later."

"I will, when the time is right. It's a delicate situation. I need this job a little longer. How long you in town for?"

"Just a few days. I'm going to stay with my sister for a bit in York. Her husband got me a job there working in his factory. I start next week."

"What happened to your old job?"

"Shut down. We all got laid off a couple months back. Did some work on the docks to tie me over."

"What happened there?" I ask, pointing to his cheek.

"Shrapnel. The craziest thing is that I think it was a German bloke that saved me. Young kid pulled me aside behind a wall. Left me there covered. I thought he was going to finish me, but he didn't. Hell of a time coming back from that. How did we make it so long? Do you ever wonder why us bastards survived when everyone else didn't?"

"Every fucking day."

"I'll keep your secret. But I better be invited to the wedding."

I laugh, feeling a little more at ease about my visitor, though that still leaves me with questions, like who was in my flat. Seems like the wrong kind of question to ask at a reunion so I hold myself back from inquiring further.

"I gotta go back. My shift doesn't end for a while. Just got away for a bit."

"Right," he replies. "Let's have a proper catch up before I head out to York. How about tomorrow night? I can meet you down in the lobby here, grab a bite, say 7:00?"

"Yea, but I'll be damned if we eat here. I know a good place."

He smiles and pushes into my shoulder, patting me once over. "You must know all the nice fancy places now. Your treat then?"

There's a weight off my shoulder, yet another one appears. I can't pinpoint what exactly it's from, but it's heavy and I just hope I can trust Jimmy to keep my secret a little longer.

Chapter 15

Ada

The hours tick by. I'm anxious to see Kasper. I remember the feeling of butterflies with my husband, but this is different. This is a longing I haven't felt before. Not just the nerves from the unknown, but a desire that's building inside of me that I feel might burst if I can't see him soon. Am I crazy to fall for a man I barely know? Love at first sight is something they only talk about in novels, but perhaps it really does exist outside of the fictional world. I feel like I see him everywhere I go, even when I know it's not him. Wishful thinking. I was hoping work would be enough to distract me today, but my attempts at erasing the images of our lustful encounter have failed me.

I'm lying on the dull green sofa in the sitting room looking around at the art that's on the walls. There's a picture of a garden that I always enjoy looking at. Something about it has always felt calming, though I don't remember when my father got this painting. Has it always been on these walls? I'm not sure. It's slightly tilted so I go over to it and straighten it out. I sit back down to stare at it and *CRASH!* It falls down, the glass from the frame splitting into pieces on the floor. I walk over to examine the nail in the wall. It's tilted up, to prevent the string from sliding off. *How the heck?* The string from the frame is still intact and I'm puzzled as to how it came off.

It would have had to get picked up off the nail for it to fall. Surely my tilting of it back to normal wouldn't have caused such a disaster.

I hear another crash and a picture on the opposite side of the wall has fallen. I don't like this picture much. It's of a basket with flowers in it but it has always seemed so dull to me. I am still left pondering how both pictures have just fallen. A cold sweeps over me and my skin lights up with goosebumps.

Such a mess. I must clean this up before he gets here.

"What have you done, pretty girl?"

"I ... Kas. These pictures." I don't know how to explain to him what just happened, or all the occurrences that seem to happen here. I didn't even hear the door open. I must have left it unlocked again, maybe subconsciously on purpose.

"Let me help you clean it up." He leaves the room and comes back with a broom, one that doesn't look familiar. He tells me to stay away from the glass while he gets to work.

"You'll never believe me when I tell you that those pictures fell all on their own, like the vase that broke before that. I swear I have a ghost following me around this house."

He looks at me with slightly furrowed brows. I wonder what he's thinking.

"Tell me about your childhood, Ada. I told you about mine. I want to know about yours."

This man has a very strange and abrupt way of getting to know someone, and yet convinces me at the same time. I indulge his curiosity.

"Well, my mother was ill. She didn't like me very much. She tried to hurt me and my father had her put away as you know. But my father was a good man. He loved me. I don't remember a lot from my childhood. I mean, I think I was happy."

"And your marriage?"

"Edward was a good man. Our marriage was full of highs and lows. He worked a lot. More than is probably good for a marriage, but we loved each other."

"And what about children? Why didn't you have any children?"

My heart beat picks up for reasons unknown and I place my hand on my stomach.

"We didn't have any children because–"

Kasper sets down the broom and dustpan and sits beside me. "Go on, love," he encourages, taking the hand from my stomach and holding it in his.

"I–" I don't know what I'm feeling but I don't like this sense of impending doom. I stare into Kasper's eyes and feel safe, but I also feel like I'm spinning, just hoping he'll catch me.

"I didn't wear protection last night."

It's true, he didn't. I didn't even think to ask. Why didn't I think to be careful?

"I can't have kids," I whisper out.

"Why not?" He pushes.

"Because... because–" I gasp, holding my hand up to my face, tears making their way into my eyes to blur my vision.

"I lost her. I lost, I lost, I lost–" I begin weeping, the fresh tears making their way down my cheek only for Kas to gently sweep them away.

"You can't have kids, because you lost your pregnancy in the Blitz in 1940, isn't that right? It was the same night Sal's was bombed and everyone in it died, except you."

"Stop it," I beg quietly.

"Your mother died here in 1916. Your father died the year before at the hands of your mother when she tried to kill you. And those pictures, they aren't yours, are they?"

"STOP!" I stand up in a panic, looking around and back at him. I need to get out of here. Where am I? I need air. I need to go. I try to leave out the front door, but it's locked. How is it bloody locked?! There's nothing to unlock from the inside. Where the fuck am I?

"Let me out!" I yell towards Kasper.

He steps up and walks towards me slowly, grabbing me from behind, gentle but firm. "Sit down, Ada. We need to talk."

"I don't want to talk. I need to get out of here. You're lying. I don't want to be around you. I want to go visit my fathers grave. I need to see him. I need him."

"Your father was buried in 1915."

"No he wasn't. He just died. I just, I was there!"

"The man you saw die was your friend Arthur Wheeler. He was the live-in caretaker here, having known about you since he befriended your mother when she was here as a patient. Quiet and friendly, you grew to enjoy the comfort of his company, but he wasn't your father. Just a figment of your desires, making him into the father of your mind's eye. Everyone here plays their part for you, Ada. And the woman who killed herself in front of you wasn't your mother. Your real mother tried to stab you with a knife while you slept, and your father, the man that wanted to protect you, tried and failed. Your mother killed him when he tried to stop her. You were six years old. Your mother did die in here, but long ago. It was said to have possibly been a heart attack. They found her lifeless body in the early hours of the morning. The woman that you claimed to have been Helen was a woman who had only been here for a short while from the second ward. She was very sick. But she wasn't Helen.

You've been in here since 1941, Ada. Your husband was the one that put you in here."

"But that can't be. I just saw Max the other day," I say in almost a whisper to myself. I rub my head to soothe my thoughts. This is too much.

"Max, your old employer, is gone. You've been in a state of delusion, reverting back to the good times in your life, a survival mechanism from your brain to keep you safe. The man you call Max is named Milo. He works in the kitchens where you volunteer. He enjoys your company from what I've been told, but he isn't who you think he is, and neither am I."

"You're scaring me!" The room is closing in on me trying to take in all this information.

"Who did I go on a date with? Who was that man?"

"It was a visiting doctor from another institution, studying some of the patients here. Since Milo and you are close, he was asked to help ease you into it. You're not the easiest person to meet for the first time."

"You're lying."

"No, Ada. For once I'm going to tell you the whole truth. I'm going to tell you something now, and I need you to stay as calm as you can. I know this is a lot, but it's the only way I can get you out of here, okay?"

I nod quickly, my body shaking from the shock I'm feeling.

"My name *is* Kasper. Jude Kasper Bailey. I'm not a doctor here. I'm a caretaker at a library, or at least I was before the war. Everything you know about me is true, except that I'm no doctor, but you are exactly who I knew you to be, everything I imagined. I need to get you out of here. But I needed to be your cure first. I think they are catching on and I don't know how much longer I've got. We need to leave, Ada. I need to take you away somewhere safe. They don't know how to help you here. But I know you see me as I see you. I know you know what's real, that we're real. Tell me you feel it." I take her hand and place it on my chest above my heart.

"I feel it," she replies. "My husband, he put me here? He left me." It's more of a statement than a question.

"Yes."

"I remember. I remember. That night I wasn't supposed to work. Edward insisted I shouldn't be working at such a job in my state but I loved it there. I made a deal with him that once I made it halfway in my pregnancy that I would stop working. I only had another week left and I stayed later that evening with Max to prepare some of the stock for the morning. We had a bomb shelter in the basement. It was safe. It was supposed to be safe. I lost my daughter. I lost her."

He's comforting me as all the memories flood back to me. I don't want to feel this pain but here it is, right in front of me.

"I *am* crazy, aren't I? Why are you still here?"

"Because I'm crazy too, peach. And you don't have to do this alone anymore. Whatever world you are in, is the world I want to be a part of."

"The books," thinking about all the clues he left me in his poems, and all the stories with their passions and tragedies.

"I read a lot. It was one of the benefits of working at a place with so many books. I'm a smart man, just not an educated one."

"You did this for me? You pretended to be a doctor to get to me? To help me?"

"Yes. I'd do anything for you. You're the only thing that has helped me survive. The least I can do is help you survive too."

"Where are we going to go?"

"Where do you want to go?"

"It doesn't matter. Maybe a small house in the countryside? Wouldn't that be swell?"

"Okay, baby. I've got some money saved up for us. It's enough to get our life started, the perks of having a doctor's paycheque."

"When?" I ask, wondering how the hell we're going to pull this off. I can't even wrap my mind around where I currently am.

"Soon. I have to sort out a few things yet."

"What if they catch you? Do they know about us?"

"No. No they don't. I'm so sorry they did this to you, baby. You're just a little lost. So am I. It's why we need each other. It's the only way we can survive this world. It's not meant for us. But we are meant for us."

He pulls me towards him, nestling me on his lap, running his hand through my hair as I rest my head on his shoulder, still shaky from his truths. The smell of his cologne is comforting, the way he holds me, a security blanket I never had. The memories all come back to me, ones I don't want to remember and I shut them out, holding onto him a little tighter.

I don't know how long we stay there for, me in his arms, but sometime in the night, I feel him carry me out of the room down the corridor into room 111. My room. *My* room. This is my room. This is my room in Huberts, where I have been since 1941.

He places me on my bed and whispers to me. "I'll be back tomorrow. Get some sleep. Tonight was a lot." He sweeps the strands of my hair off my face, and glides his hand down my cheek, staring at me with tired eyes before he disappears into the night.

CHAPTER 16

Kasper

I check on Ada first thing in the morning. She has a group meeting today, and I'm not sure how the day will go given everything I spilled to her last night.

I peek into her room in the morning and see she is still asleep. Morning rounds don't start for another hour, and I quietly sneak into her room before anyone can see me.

I close the door behind me and sit on the edge of Ada's bed, staring at her peaceful face. I wonder what's going through her mind as she dreams. I can't watch her all day and I don't want to wake her, but if I could, I wouldn't leave this spot until I was the first one she saw every time she woke.

I go to slip out and just as I'm turning the door handle, I hear her stir.

"Don't leave yet, Kas," she whispers out.

I turn to her as she stretches in her single bed by the window, the sun peaking in and setting a glow on her soft skin. She rubs her eyes, and settles her head sideways on her pillow facing me.

"Are we leaving today?" she asks in a gentle whisper.

"No pretty girl, not today. But soon."

"I remember when I was a girl, I used to listen to classical music. I'd wake up to it every morning. The home I stayed in was for kids like me, lost and alone, but they had this phonograph in the sitting room. They would never use it, but I found the old records in a dusty box one day when I was rifling through old books. Brahms was the one that I snuck into my room first. I hid it under my clothes and in the early morning, before the others woke up, I'd sneak into that room and play it, dance to it. It was my little peace that I had just for myself. And one day, I got caught. Sister Charlotte said I was a nuisance and she took the record and she smashed it against the wall, and it fell to pieces in front of me. I cried for so long without that music. For someone that stood with the voice of God, she sure knew how to put me in my own hell. Today, you are my Brahms."

There's a knock at the door that catches my attention before I can respond to Ada. I panic for a moment, then open the door to see Nurse Arden standing there.

"Oh uhh, I didn't realize you were in yet. I was just coming in to _"

I cut her off before she can reply. "You're not supposed to be on this ward. I think you should leave before you upset my patient."

"Why are you here, Doctor?" She looks back and forth between us, the suspicion in her eyes showing as I try to block Ada's view of the nurse. The last time she saw Nurse Arden, she tried to strangle her. I don't want to trigger anything else with Ada that will put her back into her delusionary state, not when we've made more progress in weeks than she has in the years before she spent in here.

"Leave now, Nurse, before I report you for insubordination."

"Sure thing, Doctor. My apologies," she says while eyeing me sharply.

"Who was that?" Ada asks.

"Nobody important, just a staff member doing morning rounds."

"Ok. Will you visit me tonight?"

"Perhaps. I've got a meeting with an old friend first."

I blow her a kiss and leave the room knowing I have a full desk of paperwork to get started on. I think I'd be good at this job if I had the opportunity to take this route in life. Luckily for me, I made my own way in this world despite my shortcomings.

Let's see what today brings.

***

"Dr. Knight, could you please wait just a second. I wanted to talk to you about your patient, Ada Thompson," Dr. Preston calls me. "I ran into her today and I have to say, whatever you've been doing, it's working. She seems calm today and lucid. I have enjoyed getting to know Ada, but it seems I don't quite have the personal touch that you have. She seems much more amenable with you."

"Yes, well, getting off her previous treatments I think have helped but mainly, I think bringing up certain triggers has helped her to regain some sense of her new reality. Just enough to let the light in, not enough to blind her to close it again."

"Well, whatever you're doing, it's working. We did find some short term success with the electroshock therapy, but she would eventually fall back into her delirium state. Perhaps you'll unlock something more. Good work."

"Thank you."

Praise from Dr. Preston is appreciated, but the only one that really matters is Dr. Wilson and his are harder to come by.

I head out on my way to meet Jimmy at his hotel. When I get there, I see him standing out front talking to someone, though I can't quite make out who it is. It looks to be a woman. I can only see the back of her head that is covered by a scarf. Jimmy waves to me and the woman scatters.

"Hey, mate. Where are you taking me?" he asks while getting in the car.

"How do you feel about steak? I know this great place around the corner."

"As long as you're paying, I'll eat just about anything."

"Who was that woman you were with?" I inquire.

"Oh just someone asking for directions," he says, looking out the window.

I don't pry any further. Something about Jimmy puts me on edge. Tonight will be a good feeler for what he really wants.

The cloudy skies that have fallen over Britain this afternoon have dimmed the lighting inside of the restaurant. White clothed round tables only half full tonight, give me a sense of relief as the quiet chatter roams the atmosphere of the quaint space.

We get a table at the back and look over our menus. I'd never think to spend such an amount on a meal. Most of my money has been squared away for safekeeping but tonight, I'm having to sugar coat this visit in hopes it's nothing more than an old loyal friend wanting to catch up.

We place our order, making small talk while we wait for our food to arrive. Jimmy dives into stories of the war, the last thing I want to talk about. It took me long enough to forget it, but I indulge his nostalgia by stepping back in time to relive some of the good moments in between all the fighting. Jimmy and I only knew each other for a short while, but there's a certain brotherhood that only happens when men are forced to be at their worst, their most feared, their most vulnerable.

We dive into our dinner; baked potatoes with a beautiful cut of meat with fried onions on top and a side of cut carrots and squash in cubes.

"So how come you don't have a girl? From what you told me, you were always a ladies man. And that scar, that's gotta attract a few lookers."

"I had a couple girlfriends when I got back. Didn't like my drinking much. It was hard when we got home. They all wanted us until they learned that our scars sunk deeper than our skin, then they ran like little mice. We risked our lives for this country, and what has it given us back? I have this pain behind my eye that never goes away. It's always there. The headaches. They get bad, blinding even. I almost put a bullet through my own head once. I didn't lose my job because of layoffs. They let me go because I missed too many days of work."

"And you've seen doctors?"

"Yea but they all say the same thing. They write me a prescription for pain medication and send me on my way. I've had blood letting which didn't do much at all. I had leeches put on me. That was sure something. I even saw a priest once. Supposed to free up evil spirits from my head. But maybe the man who had a building fall on him and still survived would understand. Maybe even help me out? My sister's husband is a good man, but he didn't pick up a single weapon in his time and I just gotta hope I can handle the job he's offering, because I doubt he'll offer it twice if I screw it up."

"I've got nothing for ya, mate. I work on my body when I can, strengthening, stretching, and keeping things limber. I don't have the headaches, but I have the body aches, the ones that run deep into my bones. Sometimes the pain in my ribs starts aching for no reason, and the one in my back. The one in my back is the worst.

Sometimes it feels like it's broken all over again. And the nightmares. They never go away. You just have to wake up and try to take on the day hour by hour and find a woman, even just one that can warm your bed, something to distract you from it. And quit the drink. Nothing good will come of it, I promise you that."

We finish up our meal, I pay the bill and we head out to the street to find the car. When I get to it, there's a note on the window folded up under my wiper. I grab the note and unfold it to read:

I know your secret.

"Did you put this here?" I ask Jimmy, throwing the note at him. He reads it himself then shakes his head, though there's something in his reply that leaves me wondering if he's holding back on me.

"It's not from me. Did you piss anyone off lately?"

"Just a nurse," I laugh lightly.

"Well you better make amends then to cover your behind."

I look around at the street to see if anyone is lingering, watching, but nobody's looking.

"When you came to my flat to look for me, did you go in my place by any chance? Someone let you in or anything of the sort?"

He looks at me inquisitively, "No, I didn't even get into the building."

"Okay, okay," I say more to myself. I'm going to have to move quicker than I thought if I'm going to have any chance of getting Ada out of that place. But first, I need to visit my angel because the night is over and I haven't yet had my dessert.

Chapter 17

Ada

I never believed in love at first sight. I believed love could be found in each person we met if we only let ourselves. Love was something to attain, something to work hard for. I found that in Edward. I loved him from friendship and I loved him as my husband. He wanted to mold me into the perfect wife, of which I was not. I wanted our marriage and I wanted independence. Someone to love my spirit and let it run free at the same time. And yet freedom is the one thing he took from me when he gave up on me.

Kasper is giving me something back, something I didn't even realize I needed. But more than that, he's proven to me that love does exist on its own. It knows no boundaries. It holds no grudges. It's ever present, maddening. Sure, love is patient and kind, and it is also irrational and unpredictable and fierce. It's unapologetic, and I've found that in him.

I know I'm sick. I know this isn't the first time I've had the fog lifted to my reality. I know these episodes of delirium as they call them might come back as they always have, but what if they don't? What if he can keep me grounded? Or what if instead, I'm dooming him, sending him to his own hell? Love is selfish as much as it's selfless even when we don't want to admit it.

I look around my somewhat barren room with only my bed, a small wardrobe and an old vanity that Edward negotiated for them to let me have, or so I was told. It's because of him I have my own room. Not everyone here does. Most have two to a room, but my behaviour was too unpredictable to room with anyone else, and so Edward made sure to make a large enough donation to the facility in order to pay off the guilt he felt from putting me in here to begin with.

He used to visit me every Saturday. We would take walks outside the yard. Towards the side of the old property are raspberry bushes, and we'd eat them when they were in season. I stopped imagining him as my husband at some point. It was harder to see him, knowing he'd abandoned me. So I made up stories in my head as to where he had gone. Sometimes it would be trips around the world to places he was writing about, or a headache he had to stay in bed for. And those stories became my reality, my little bits of comfort to try and make good out of my situation. But the problem with that is that I'm a little too good at putting myself into a different life. It's the one I get to be in control of, and nobody can take that from me. If I keep my mind busy, then I don't have to re-live my truth.

Sometimes I help out in the kitchens here. I've always been a good cook, a skill we had to learn in the home I was in. The nuns there said if we had a chance in this world, we'd better learn to become good wives, and they taught us the skills that were needed to run a household. They made us fear God and fear man, and yet I feared myself more. The brain is capable of extraordinary things. None of which they were equipped to handle, but somehow I made it out. I worked, I struggled, I worked more. Max was my saving grace. He gave me the first job I really enjoyed, one I didn't dread going to in part because of his company. He was a male figure I never had growing up, and even though I was already an adult when I met him, he was always protective over me, so I knew that I trusted his judgment when he pushed me to go out with Edward.

Edward knew I was a handful, but he wanted me despite it. How could I not say yes to such an offer, when I knew the odds had been stacked against me.

I saw things sometimes as a child. The nuns used to make me pray more to rid my demons. Edward, on the other hand, would calm me down but he never believed me. Nobody ever believed me. I see things that I know aren't supposed to be real, but they must be. Pictures don't just fall off of walls. Rings don't just appear. The voices, the footsteps that I know others hear as well, are real. But they don't believe us.

I can't help but wonder whether Kasper will see me for what I am. Will he believe me, or will I be fighting against the inevitable? Will these visions only ever be for me?

I'm laying in bed deep in my doubtful thoughts when I hear my door open. Kasper walks in, closing the door behind him quietly. I sit up excitedly. The smile on his face is enough to light up the entire darkness of this room.

"Get some shoes on. I want to take you somewhere. You're going to have to be quiet though."

I slip on a pair of flats, wrap my robe around me to cover my white nightgown, and hold onto his hand.

We slip out the door and he puts his finger up to his mouth, gesturing for us to be quiet. We move down the corridor and into his back office. He closes the door behind us and I'm in awe with the sight in front of me. He has a table cloth draped over the walnut stained desk, candles lit on both sides, with two plates and cutlery and from the ceiling are draped purple wisteria vines covering the old white chipped paint.

"How did you–" My words fail to come out.

"Don't worry about it. Tonight, you and I are going to have a proper date. Now, if you would please have a seat." He pulls my chair out for me and I sit down. It's the first time I've been in this office that I recall it being such a pleasant atmosphere.

He moves across to the chair adjacent to me and lifts up a basket with various prepared foods. "Now I did have a little help. I'm afraid I'm not much of a cook, but my landlady is. For you, my love, we have roast beef cooked to tender perfection, yorkshire pudding and the finest gravy I've ever tasted with a side of green beans draped with butter garlic."

He removes a large glass casserole dish with the contents of the beef and green beans, unwrapping the yorkshire pudding wrapped in a towel and the gravy in a smaller glass jar. He serves out the food for us, then continues to pour us each a glass of water in two wine glasses he places on the table, wrapped from the basket.

"A toast. To the rest of our lives."

I smile at him, cheers his glass, and sip the water.

"What if someone comes in?"

"No one will. They don't come down here during the night. I've worked many nights in this office, I assure you."

"I've never had dinner at this hour before. You went through all this trouble for me?" I say, still surprised at his attempts to give us some normalcy.

"I'd go to war for you again if it meant I could put that very smile on your face," he replies.

I take a bite of the roast beef covered in gravy, and he's right in saying it's the best I've ever tasted. I close my eyes savouring the rich flavours. We don't talk much during the meal, but it doesn't feel awkward. The food here isn't normally that great. This feels like a luxury. I'm not sure how this place is funded, only that repairs haven't been done in a very long time and the food is mediocre at best. Porridge for breakfast gets old very fast. Sometimes we have bread, and as a rarity, jam. My peach chutney comes around once a year and the kitchen help usually chips in to buy the peaches themselves. I'm grateful for the small givings here. I can't say all the staff are generous.

The second floor on the left wing is the women's first ward where I am, and on the right wing is the second ward where there are more shorter term patients. Most of the women on my ward will be here for life, the same as me. We aren't allowed on the grounds unless supervised, but there's a decent view from some of the windows up here. Most of our treatments are done on the first floor, and there are staff bedrooms for those that stay for longer shifts. It's a smaller facility compared to others in the country.

"How did you do it?" I ask Kasper. "How did you manage to get the job here?"

"To be honest, sometimes I'm still surprised it worked. It took months of research, a lot of books, and finding the right people to forge the papers I needed. I saw an opportunity and took it. Dr. Winston Knight went to France to help with medical aid and never came home. It was the perfect means to my new identity if I could pull it off. It was far enough away from where he was from that nobody would hear of him showing back up, but his name backed up the credentials in case they checked here. If anything, it would buy me some time. I don't expect my lie to hold out for much longer."

"How does one in such a profession even end up there? I mean, there were enough problems on our soil without having to leave across the sea."

"The minds of men were wounded as much as their bodies after the war. Shell shock, war neurosis. Not an easy fix. There were hospitals set up just for that, and thank God for it."

"I can't imagine. What was it like? I mean I know what it was like here, but what was it like there? Is that okay to ask?"

"On the best of days it was hell, most days it was worse. I had no reason to live. No one to come back home to. These men would pull out letters from their loved ones, pictures, little pieces of their history and they would have hope. And then they would die in front of me and any bit of hope we all had died with them too. I've seen things I'll never be able to erase. I was ready to die. I begged the grim reaper to let it be me and not them but it was always them and never me."

"What did you do, your position?"

"Well, most of us started off with the same rank, but I made it to Sergeant before I was nearly blown to bits. A German tank came in, took out a building I was in."

He stares away from me blankly, almost as if he is reliving it.

"You and I both then, except it wasn't a tank. It was a plane."

That breaks him free from his daze and he's looking at me again empathetically, realizing how similar our situations had been during what should have been our final moments.

"And yet here we are. Together," he says.

We finish up our meals, licking all the last bits of gravy off our plates before he tidies up, making the desk look like a desk once again.

"I should take you back." He's barely looking at me in the eyes when he says it.

I don't want this night to be over just yet and I know he doesn't either. We walk down the corridor and just as we are halfway to my room, a night staff nurse's footsteps alert us in surprise.

"Shit," Kasper whispers, standing in front of me. We hear the click of her heels making their way closer to us and Kas pulls me into a small room on the side. The light is off so I don't see where we are. He presses me against the door and tells me not to make a sound. We hear the footsteps pass us by and both breathe a sigh of relief.

"Where are we?" I ask.

He flicks on the light and we notice we are standing in the maintenance closet.

"This looks familiar," he says.

The small room has wooden shelves lining the longest side. At the end of the room is a sink with old brooms and mops and an aluminum bucket. On the opposite side, there is a small desk, no bigger than what you would see in a classroom, with a wooden chair and a tin ashtray sitting on the desk. I've been in this room before, many times even when visiting Arthur.

"Feels like home," he smirks.

We both laugh a little and then his look gets more serious, more stern. I've seen what happens when his deep blues look at me like that. The hunger in them is terribly intimidating yet it excites me to no end.

"Doctor, I think we should get back," I suggest, knowing damn well we aren't moving from this room.

"Right, my favourite little patient needs her beauty sleep. Tell me, angel, how would you feel about a little therapy to help you dream happy thoughts?"

He pushes me back into the door, his strong body pressing into my small form and connects our lips with intensity. He takes my hands and pins them above my head, his one hand large enough to grip both my wrists while running his fingers down the inside of my arm with his free hand. He pulls open my robe, seeing the nightgown underneath.

"Undress," he commands.

I shake my head no in defiance, just to egg him on a little. He turns me around in a sudden motion, pulls my hips back and smacks my behind, then pulls my backside against his chest while his hand lightly wraps around my throat.

"Do you defy me? Your doctor? There are consequences to that."

"And what would those consequences be?" I push.

"Unimaginable pleasure," he whispers in my ear.

"Then by all means, Doctor, do your worst."

He pulls my robe down letting it hit the ground then rips my cotton nightgown down the back, letting it fall along with it until I'm standing with both pieces of fabric by my feet, naked in his sight. He turns me around and takes me in, slowly dropping his gaze down my body.

"Your body, Ada, is something of most men's dreams, but I get to be the one to live it, to breathe you in, to feel the softness of your touch."

I pull off his suit jacket, and unbutton his shirt. He helps me by removing it off of him. He then watches me while I unbutton his trousers and the layer below them, pushing them down off his legs until his dick springs free, greeting me at full stance.

Kasper places his hand against my cheek and meets his lips to mine, his tongue finding its way in. He walks to the back of the small room to get the wooden chair and places it in the middle of the room.

"Sit," he demands.

I do as he asks and before I know it, he's kneeling in front of me, spreading me wide and pulling my hips towards him so I'm slightly off the edge of the chair.

"This is mine now, angel," he says before moving his head in between my legs and licking my centre. I know we have to be quiet but he's going to make that difficult for me. I silence a moan, breathily saying his name while he continues moving his tongue around me, like he's still licking the gravy off the plate. He sticks a finger inside of me without warning. I'm caught off guard, but in the best of ways as my pleasure starts to build. He adds in a second finger and my head falls back while I grasp onto his hair, tugging at the light strands on the top. Just when I think I'm about to come apart, he stops, pulling away.

"Don't you dare stop," I protest.

"That's what happens when you don't listen, peach. You're going to have to work for it now. Stand up."

I do as he says, desperate for his touch once more.

"Do you want to be a good patient for me now, sweet girl?"

"Yes, I'll be good. Please."

He smiles, biting his lip in the process and changes places with me, sitting down on the chair.

"Your seat is nice and warm for you," he says, pulling my thighs towards him until I'm straddling him, his cock, hard and red against me. He leans in and kisses my neck, softly at first, but then bites into me like he wants a taste of my flesh, blood and all. I start grinding up on him, inviting him to continue the small sensations of pain along my skin. He bites into my shoulder, followed up by a small gentle kiss, then lifts me onto his cock. I adjust myself first then slowly start to sit into him, the stretching sensation a familiar one from before, but the pleasure that emanates from us is just as he said, unimaginable.

I grind up and down on him, my feet barely able to touch the ground. His palms grip my behind, helping me with the movement to deepen our contact.

We get a rhythm going while I run my hand through the back of his hair.

"God, Ada. Where have you been all my life?"

"Waiting for you," I reply back.

He pulls my ass cheeks harder into him and the both of us, nearly out of breath, collapse when the back chair leg breaks off and sends us tumbling backward.

We both stare at each other shocked for a moment.

"Are you okay?" he asks.

I just start laughing, and he follows. He puts his hand over my mouth to try and quiet the sounds, the shaking of our abdomens from our laughter only increasing the pleasures with us both still connected. It's one of those uncontrollable belly laughs you get that you don't seem to have much control over, both of us only making it worse for the other.

He turns me over onto my back, moving in between my legs on the cement floor and the change of position brings my attention back to our erotic activity.

"You're going to get us caught," he says, thrusting hard into me. "I wonder if they'd let us finish." Another hard thrust.

"Kas, don't ever stop surprising me," I say.

He stops for a second staring into my eyes, leans down to kiss me on the forehead and then the lips.

"I'll never stop fighting for you." *Thrust.* "I'll never stop pursuing you." *Thrust.* "I'll never stop surprising you." *Thrust.*

He pushes into me with a power I haven't yet felt, the intensity of his stare deepening, his forehead wrinkling with his sudden seriousness.

"Don't you dare look away from me," he says with a dark tone.

I don't know where it comes from, but it does and I know this is the right moment.

"I love you, Jude Kasper Bailey."

His look of surprise or relief, I can't figure out which one, softens his features for a second. His eyes widen as if in grief. "Ada. I love you into lunacy, and yet it is the very thought of our love that makes me sane."

He picks up his pace and the feeling below builds once more bringing with it a sense of surrender that I've only ever experienced with him. The feeling of security, of safety resides within us as we are one and I want nothing more than to stay here in this little room forever just so we can be as we are.

"Keep looking at me, baby." I bring my eyes back to his, the distraction from our pleasure pulling me away only for a moment. He holds his palm onto my cheek, a bead of sweat moving down the side of his face, and I melt into his stare as my orgasm washes over me.

"That's it, love. Fuck."

His palm on my cheek moves over to my mouth to quiet my cries of gratification and just as I think my orgasm is tapering down, his cock pulses inside of me, the small contractions prolonging my own pleasure as his come releases, the warmth a welcome feeling.

Kasper gets a panicked look on his face and cups his hand tighter over my mouth, leaning into my ear. "Don't make a sound. Someone's coming."

Yea, both of us.

He moves slowly inside me as our bodies relax into each other. I hear footsteps coming again that stop right at the door.

The light. We turned it on when we came in here. This is it. We're going to get caught. Someone is going to come in here to shut it off and find us naked on the cement floor, Kasper's bare arse, the first thing they see. But the footsteps start up again, moving down the corridor.

He releases his hand from my mouth and lets out a small laugh.

"That was close. Too close. We need to get you back before our luck runs out."

We hurriedly get dressed and just as we are about to leave the room, a loud noise comes from behind us, a broom falls over and hits the aluminum bucket, making a ruckus.

"You saw that, right?" I ask.

"Yea, I saw that. Maybe it was...I dunno." He puts the chair back in the corner, attempting to put the leg back on but it's no use. It's broken beyond repair.

Kasper shuts off the light, and checks the corridor before we start to move. By the time I get back into my room, it's past 1:00 a.m.

I wish he could stay with me for the night, but of course he can't. We're already breaking so many rules.

"Kas, before you go. If we only ever had tonight, I would die happy."

He places a soft kiss on my lips, brushing my hair through his hand.

"If you go first, you better come back as a ghost and haunt me until it's my turn. I'll do the same for you, because I don't think I can live this life without your presence. Once I get you out of here, I'm putting a ring on that finger. How does that sound, Mrs. Bailey?"

"Sounds perfect," I respond, a tear about to shed from my eye.

He sneaks away, leaving me alone in my room, yet it is the least lonely I have felt in my entire life knowing he'll be here for me tomorrow.

CHAPTER 18

Kasper

When I walk into the building the next morning, Nurse Arden is staring at me strangely. I'm 10 minutes early, as I always am on any given day, but she won't take her eyes off me. I ignore her and instead, as scheduled, head to our employee meeting in the rec hall where they run physician meetings once a month to discuss patient cases.

"Ah, Dr. Knight, pleased to see you," Dr. Wilson greets me.

"Yes, good morning."

"Before we get started today, I'd like to have a word with you." He gestures to me over to the corner of the room. "Nothing to worry about, it's just that St. Anne's is running short on staff this week. Two of their doctors have fallen ill and they have asked if I might be able to lighten their load until their return. It would only be for the week but you see, I have so much work to catch up on myself and that is why I recommended you. It's a small hospital, but the department for mental health is well kept and the patients there have more mild cases, mainly short term rehabilitation visits. You can head over after the meeting today. Just check in with the main office when you get there and they'll take care of you, issue you an ID and you'll be set for the week."

I haven't been here long, but still long enough to know this isn't something I can say no to. Dr. Wilson is the lead doctor of this institution and I would do well not to question his authority if I want to keep my position here.

"Of course, I'd be happy to fill in. A little change of scenery can do us some good, I think."

"Hmm, I agree."

I need to talk to Ada before I go. She'll be expecting me since I won't be needed here for the week, I won't be able to make any night time calls. This throws my plan off track a bit, but it's only a week.

We discuss our patient cases, being praised for my current work, specifically with Ms. Thompson where Dr. Preston speaks highly of me. They are weary of how long this period of calm will last given the history of her psychotic relapses. Perhaps they shouldn't send me away for a week if they think I'm doing so well with one of their hardest cases. The last thing I need is a setback.

Ada is in the kitchen when I find her.

"Good day, Doctor. Anything I can help you with?" she asks, winking.

"Actually, yes. I'm being sent to St. Anne's for the week to relieve some staffing issues and I will not be in attendance, but I wanted to let you know in case you were wondering where your favourite doctor has disappeared to. I'll check up on you upon my return."

Ada's face falls but she nods. "Yes of course. I hope you have a good week. I look forward to our next counseling session when I get back."

"That's what you're calling it now," I whisper. "Dr. Wilson will be taking your case for the week. I'll be in touch should anything come up."

"Why not Dr. Preston? I much prefer his company."

"It's out of my control, I'm afraid. I need you to keep your head clear for me, okay?"

"Okay." She runs her hand over mine softly, pulling away before anyone can see.

I get to my car and there is a note on my windshield in a small envelope. I open it to see a blank card.

I'm sorry.
-Jimmy

What the hell does he have to be sorry about? Maybe that he left without saying goodbye? Maybe something else. I can't focus on this now. I have to be at St. Anne's hospital within the hour and it's on the other side of the city. Not only is it pulling me further away from Ada, it's wreaking havoc on my plans. Ada and I were supposed to be out of here by the end of the week, and now I have to postpone it. I don't like this feeling. She needs me and this is going to feel like the longest week of my life.

When we leave here, we'll have different names and different lives. In two days time, I'll pick up our papers for our new identities. I never thought I'd return to France, but it'll give us a new start. I've got enough put away to get us a small flat to rent until I find work. It's not going to be easy and it won't be much, but it'll be enough. We are enough, her and I.

***

"Dr. Wilson, you've asked to see me?" The week at St. Anne's was long and tedious. I missed Ada every single moment of the day. I went years without knowing her, and now even going a day without seeing her feels like torture. When I walk into the room, there are two security guards standing in his office.

"Sir? What is this about?"

"Have a seat, *Knight*." He emphasizes the Knight in a strange way and my stomach is rolling with a sense of consternation that I haven't felt in a long time.

I sit down at the desk, both guards unmoving at the back wall behind me.

"Well, why don't you tell me?"

The look of confusion and dread falls onto my face for a split second and I know he sees it before it drops.

"I'm not sure what you mean, sir."

"Sure you do. Inappropriate relations with a patient is not only against the rules, but against the law. However–" he puts his hand out in a stop gesture. He pulls out a file from his desk and opens it up. Inside is a picture of a man with the name Winston Knight. "Impersonating a doctor will put you behind bars for years to come." He motions for the guards behind me. "Gentleman, you'll wait here with him until the police show up. They are already on their way."

Something inside of me flicks on. Fight or flight. This is it. I'm not leaving here without Ada. I push the desk towards Dr. Wilson, throwing him back. The guard on my right– furthest from the door– moves first, trying to push me down by my shoulder, but I stand in response and thrash my elbow into his face, making him grab his nose. The second guard moves in. I pick up the chair I was sitting on and smash it over him, but he grabs the legs to lessen the blow. I kick him in the gut, causing him to lean forward then knock my fist into the side of his head, throwing him over. I sprint out of the office, closing the door behind me, and run down to room 111. Ada's not in there.

"STOP HIM!" Nurse Arden yells out.

"Insubordination nurse, get back up to the second ward!" I yell, running down to the rec room where I see Ada in conversation with another woman.

"Doctor! You're back," she says to me with a look of concern that coats her face right after she sees my distress."

"We need to go, Ada. Now!"

She nods quickly, grabbing my hand.

"STOP!" Two more security guards are running down the corridor.

"Fuck! Hold on tight, baby." Luckily I still have my keys. I take a left at the corridor making our way down to the set of stairs that leads down to the first floor. They'll be expecting that, but I have a better plan. We run down the stairs, being careful not to trip with our speed, until we hit the basement. It's used mostly for storage and the conditions down here are awful, damp and musty, likely making it a perfect thriving space for rats.

"Where are we going?" Ada asks.

"You're just going to have to trust me."

There's a boiler room at the end of the hall and above it, a small window, just large enough for us to fit through. The glass is cracked and I make no attempts to save it. I take a piece of metal piping that's laying on the side and knock the window out, taking off my blazer to clean up the glass.

"Okay, you first."

I lift Ada up by the hips while she grabs onto the frame, pulling herself up with my help.

"Check down here!" I hear being yelled.

"Go baby, we gotta move quick."

Ada gets herself up and now it's my turn. I lift myself up and barely squeeze through it, hitting my back against the top of the frame while I wiggle my way out. A piece of remaining glass I missed from the corner scrapes down the side of my back, leaving a large gash through my button down shirt.

"You're hurt!" Ada says, staring at the blood leaking through the white fabric.

"I'll be okay. We gotta run."

My car is only 200 feet away past the gates and chances are, they'll see us before we get there, but it's a chance we have to take.

"Hold my hand and run as fast as you can. Don't look back, no matter what."

"Okay." Ada is shaking and pale, the nerves firing through both of us.

"Now!"

"There he is!" I hear from the boiler room as we take off. A guard from the front of the building is running towards us and there's already one waiting for us at the gate.

He's got a baton out and waiting for me, but I'm bigger than him and he looks frightened by my approach. He attempts to swing the baton at my head, but I grab it and throw him to the ground, giving us just enough time to open the rod iron gates.

I re-grab Ada's hand and run with her for dear life.

"Get in!" I unlock the passenger seat then run around to mine, jumping in and starting the car just seconds before the guard gets to the car, smacking the back of it as the engine turns on. I pull out, my tires screeching, and get to the exit of the lot, the police car pulling in just as we are leaving. I act casual, hiding my panicked face before taking off, hoping they won't notice who we are. I drive until we get to my flat, parking on the side street just off from it and get out of the car. Ada follows.

"We just need to grab one thing and we'll be gone before they know it."

The papers and money I've been saving are tucked away in that drawer and it's all we need in order to flee and start our new lives.

When we get into the building, I notice my door is slightly ajar.

"Stay close," I say.

We walk into the flat and it's an absolute mess, like someone has been looking for something. The sofa has been cut into, the cupboards open with broken ceramic layering the floor, and the bedroom. *Dammit not the bedroom!*

My nightstand is open, the papers from the top drawer scattered around. I go to the bottom compartment and push it open and it's gone.

"FUCK! God dammit!" I yell out.

"It doesn't matter, Kasper. Look at me." She grabs my hands with her palms pulling my face towards her. "It doesn't matter. Whatever it is. Let's just go. We'll figure it out. We have each other. That's all we need. Please! Let's go."

She's right. We can't stay here longer. They'll be expecting that. I take Ada's hand.

"I didn't mean to let you down. I'm sorry, peach. We'll come up with another plan. Let's go!"

I walk into the living room to see Ms. Turner.

"They came by half an hour ago. You better leave before they come back. I didn't see you. Now hurry!"

I don't deserve Ms. Turner's sympathy, and I'm grateful she's not asking questions.

"Thank you," I say to her before pulling Ada with me to leave. We get to the front of the building and see a police car parked out front.

"There's a door at the back of the building. Come on."

We head down the main hall past the stairwell to a heavy wooden door. I push it open and *WHACK!* A wooden baton comes down on my head, knocking me down, and then another.

"No!" Ada yells. A second officer grabs her and pulls her back.

"Don't touch her!" I yell out.

"You be quiet now." A third whack with the baton on my back paralyzes me for a second. A pair of cuffs grip around my wrist and I'm trying to fight but I can't move, the officer now with his boot on my head.

"Angel, I love you. I'll come back for you. I promise I'll find a way!"

I'm in more agony than I ever have been but it's not my body this time, it's my heart. We were so close! We were so damn close.

"Please, let him go!" I hear Ada cry. "Please. I need him! I love you Kasper. Don't leave me."

"I'm not leaving you. I'll never leave you."

Tears are running down both our faces. Another officer shows up to take Ada, while the other two take me to their car.

"You sick bastard," his irish accent filters through as he throws me in the cab of the vehicle. "Stealing a patient, are ya? We'll see about that. You won't be seeing her again. Pretty thing she is, but not for you. Don't worry. I'll visit her while you're busy behind bars."

He slams the car door behind me. I'm broken. My soul is broken. But I'm not giving up. I'll never give up, not even when I take my last breaths will I give up. Not while I'm six feet buried in the ground will I give up. Ada is mine, and I will have justice.

Part II

Chapter 19

Kasper

7 Months Later

The courtroom is filled, the sounds of voices echoing around me in argument regarding the verdict.

"Well, there you have it. It's the best we could have hoped for," my barrister, Mr. Clarke, comments.

No, the best we could have hoped for would be to see this for what it is. A woman needing to break free of the cage a dead man put her in. Instead, they're putting me in a cage too. Only a psychotic man would pretend to be a doctor to be near the love of his life that he found from a photo of when he was nearly on his deathbed. That's what the barrister argued on my behalf to escape a worse fate of being sent to prison. They're sending me to Stanfield instead, a psychiatric hospital where they specialize in treatment of cases like mine: wrecked from war, unstable in society. I'm not wrecked. I found my remedy. She's at Huberts, where they won't give me any updates because I'm not family. I'm not anyone. Each day, I die a little more without her. The scar on my back reminds me of just how close we were to getting away. I kick myself every time I look in the mirror. I should have done it sooner. Fuck the paperwork. I could have taken her somewhere safe and waited.

I still don't know who ratted me out. Was it Jimmy? Nurse Arden? Or maybe Dr. Wilson. They don't understand us. How could they? Ada and I have a rare love. People don't understand rare love. They only understand societal love, the kind that puts on a show. I don't even have her picture anymore, only the images in my head that I refuse to let fade.

Two officers come behind me, putting my cuffs back on and motion for me to follow them.

"Listen, it's only 9 years. It could be worse. And if you're on good behavior and get right in the head, you'll get out earlier. You just need to prove that Ada was a mistake. But a moment of relapse will not help your case, Jude," Mr. Clarke says.

I'm not Jude anymore. Jude died in France in 1944. To her, I'm Kasper. That's the only name I want to be called. They might as well sentence me to life, because Ada will never be a mistake.

The two officers lead me outside where there is a vehicle waiting to bring me back to the jail I've been staying in for the last 7 months. Placed in a barren cell, I've had nothing to do but wither away with a cellmate named Carson, whose crimes are much worse than my own. I'm told I'll be transferred to Stanfield in a couple days. Of course, I've tried to plan my escape on more than one occasion. There's only so much one can do to not lose their mind while awaiting their demons. I made a promise to Ada, and I'm about to bargain with the devil to keep that promise.

***

Mornings begin at Stanfield the same monotonous way each day with a roll call, standing beside our beds in the large occupied room.

Unlike Huberts, where patients have their own rooms, here we're hoarded like animals into one space, reminding me of the days at the makeshift hospital I was sent to recover in during the war.

My bedmate is named Archie, though I've nicknamed him Archer for throwing his fork towards one of the nurses here to get her attention. He's a bit of a nutter but mostly harmless.

After roll call, we gather in the eating room where white tables line the length of the wall in rows throughout. The food here reminds me of what they serve patients at Huberts, but more bland and with never any jam for the bread they offer us. The stew we had last night was insipid and watery with only a couple pieces of meat in each bowl. The porridge this morning was no better, a little more gritty than yesterday's.

Most of the men here have scars from the war, but not all fought. Some of the younger boys here are locked up for different reasons, yet they have the same problematic tendencies that the courts deemed to be unfit for their freedom. I haven't heard all their stories, though I've been told of a couple. One is in here to fix his inappropriate thoughts about other men, and another for stealing, instigated by voices he heard. I can hear him at night sometimes, talking to himself. Nighttime is rarely quiet here. There's always something eventful happening, even if it's just the screams from our night terrors.

"Do ya think she'd go for a bloke like me?" Archie asks.

He has flame red hair and pale skin, with freckles covering over the likes of him. He's about five years younger than me with a thin frame but an inch taller than me, and is here because of something called melancholia.

I was hesitant to make connections here, but I'm going to need them if I'm going to find a way to escape this place. My own nightmares have returned since my arrest, and the sooner I get out of here, the better.

"She might if she's as crazy as the rest of us fools."

Archie laughs and slaps me in the shoulder. "You gonna eat that?"

I hand him the remains of porridge from my bowl. I'm still not one to eat breakfast but I've been forcing myself, if only to show the doctors here that I'm cooperating.

"Hey Nurse," I yell out. The young nurse with short brown hair strides over to us, blushing slightly at me while trying to remain with a stiff composure.

"Archer here wants a bite of ya. Best to stay away from him now."

The nurse looks over at Archie, who is looking down and shaking his head in embarrassment.

"I'm sorry, Nurse. He's a daft fool this one. Ignore him."

"You boys behave now. I'd hate to report you to Dr. Forrester for your insolence," she says, walking away but peering back for a last glance at us.

"I know what you need, a swift kick in the behind if you ask me," Archie spits back at me.

I laugh, knowing it's all good fun. Trying to make light out of the situation I'm in is all I can do from losing my real damn mind.

"You hear about him?" Archie says pointing to one of the biggest guys here. He must be at least 6 and a half feet tall, making my 6 ft stature look small. He's a beast, one I wouldn't mind having on my side when it comes to me getting out of here.

"What's his story?" I ask.

"I heard he killed a guy."

"Haven't most of us in this room though?"

"Nah, this is worse. Apparently his sister ran off with a kraut. Of course, the family wasn't having it. He went after them. Found them bunked up in some hostel and killed him."

"Why's he here then? Seems like a prison crime if you ask me," I say.

"Because that's not the worst of it. Story goes that he tied his sister up and made her watch. He cut open the guy's insides and started eating his heart to teach her a lesson."

I'm sickened by the thought of how vile another human can be, and more so whether the story is actually true.

"I guess that nurse better look out for more than just you for that bite, huh?"

The whistle sounds, signaling the end of our meal, and now we get to spend the next hour walking the grounds. Unlike Huberts, this place is secure all the way around the facility with barbed wire fences; another obstacle in my way of escaping this place. But it won't deter me from my life's mission.

"Come on mate," I motion to Archie in the large killer's direction. "Time to make a new friend."

CHAPTER 20

Ada

My mother's demon visits me night after night, standing in the corner, taunting me with her words. Last night was worse. She tore through my wardrobe, ripped apart my books and told me I would be alone forever and that he wasn't coming to get me. I haven't cried like that since Kasper left. I don't know what happened to him. Max told me he got sent away for a new job. But Kasper would never just leave me like that. He loves me.

I feel more dazed today. Of course I snuck a bit of my fathers gin last night. That's probably why. I thought I'd go visit his grave today, but my neighbour has stopped by for a visit. It's such a nice day out and I'd hate to be inside all day but I know he's just worried about me.

"How've you been feeling, Ada?" Mr. Preston asks me. He's been coming to visit me more often lately. I think he knows I'm struggling. Beverly stopped by a few days ago and invited me to another luncheon, but I'm not feeling very social these days so I don't plan on going. I've got too much on my mind, most of that of course being Kas.

"I don't feel quite like myself," I reply. "I haven't been sleeping well. My head is a bit foggy. I don't feel whole. Oh, silly me for complaining. I must sound like such a whinger. I apologize. Please tell me how your grandson is doing? Is he still the smartest boy in his class?"

"Trying to change the subject are we? How about you tell me about that man of yours. I know he really had an effect on you."

"Oh Mr. Preston, you have no idea. I've never felt anything like it before. He made me feel like... me. He understood me in a way no one else could. I know he lied to me. He told me he worked at Huberts as a doctor, and I think he was doing it to impress me, but I didn't need that to fall for him. Max said he got caught lying about his job and was let go, but I know he'll come back for me. He has to, right?"

"Why would you think he would come back for you? Sounds like you put him in quite the predicament. It's not very lady like to lead a man on like that."

The harshness of his tone has me pulling back. Mr. Preston has never been one to judge me. In fact he's been a wonderful listener but I don't appreciate his statement.

"When you met your wife, how did it feel?"

"Well, she's a wonderful woman. She made me very happy."

"But it was more than happiness, wasn't it? Like a flame between the two of you that only grew the closer you got? And when you are away from her, like a hot coal, just waiting to be ignited upon her arrival. Isn't that how love feels?"

"I wouldn't say that. I think love is more like the fireplace. A sturdy construction no matter what burns in the middle."

"That doesn't sound as exciting," I comment.

He laughs slightly. "No, it's not supposed to be. It's there when things are ashy and dried up, and it's there for comfort on cold nights. But it's strong, like a marriage should be."

"I suppose. Maybe Edward was my fireplace. But with Kasper, it's different. I'm not sure there is a metaphor that could describe him."

"Try."

"Alright, well–" I pause for a moment, gathering my thoughts. "He's like a star. You see, most stars we see are so much brighter than they appear. We only see what the night sky will allow us to see, specks of gold in the distance. But he's so much more than that. I see him for what he really is. The sun of a whole other world that revolves around me, that warms me, that comforts me, that brightens my darkest thoughts. Each night I look out my window and I know that even when the clouds cover the sky, he's there trying to look down on me, the same as me looking up at him. You don't have to understand our love, Mr. Preston. We do."

"I see. Well, Ada. I better get going now. Perhaps I'll stop in next week. Thank you for the visit."

I walk Mr. Preston to the door and sit back on the dull green couch, looking up at my favourite painting on the wall. I get the strangest feeling for a second, a familiarity I can't put my finger on. It's slightly tilted, so I get up and set it right. *That's better.* It's missing the glass from the frame, and a sense of deja vu runs through me. Suddenly the room gets cold, goosebumps trail along my arms and I hear a crash. I look behind me at a picture that has fallen off the wall. It's a small one of a teacup with a kitten inside of it. I go over to the picture, perplexed by the sudden crash and attempt to gather the glass when –

Kasper

I gasp, my hand slapping over my mouth. I look around the room in a panic, noticing the blue chipped paint and emptiness of the space.

"NO!" I yell.

I get up and run to the door, whipping it open and stand in the corridor of the facility.

"I need to get out of here!" I say. "What did you do with him!" Dr. Wilson is rushing over to me.

"Now, Ada. Calm down."

"Calm down? Calm down?! Get me the hell out of here! Where is he? I need to see him. Where did they take him? Please!"

I'm practically hysterical, but how can they blame me? They hold me prisoner here when the only person that can make me feel any sense of sanity is the one man they won't let me see.

"Ada, we've been through this, the same as last week, the same as the week before. Kasper is at another facility getting the help he needs."

"He doesn't need help! He just needs me. You awful man! How could you..." I trail off. Tears are streaming down my face and I'm pushing my fists against Dr. Wilson's chest.

"Time to sleep," Nurse Arden says beside me.

I feel a prick and then my vision goes blurry. I lost the fight. I lost him.

CHAPTER 21

Roy

The walls are dull and worn here with an eeriness that speaks of dark history. This place has been standing since the mid-1800's, and I doubt it has had much of a clean up since. I'll be working on the second floor, specifically ward one for the longer term problematic patients. This place should be a cakewalk next to Broadmoar. A decade of that place will wear one down. It just so happened I heard about an opening here and took the opportunity to apply for the position. A fresh start is exactly what I need after the mess I just got out of from back home.

"Excuse me miss, I was wondering where I might find Dr. Wilson at this hour. I'll be starting here today," I say to the nurse with dark hair.

"Oh you must be Dr. Rosco. Nice to meet you. I'm Nurse Arden. I work on this floor as well. Dr. Wilson's office is down the corridor to the right. I'll take you there."

I'm at least thirty years her superior, and yet that doesn't stop her from batting those eyelashes at me. I'm not one for being manipulated, and I take my work seriously.

"So I heard you were coming from Broadmoar. Is it as bad there as they say it is?"

"No," I reply. "It's worse."

The nurse knocks on the door for me and opens it to let Dr. Wilson know I've arrived.

"Come in Rosco," he calls out.

I don't appreciate the informality given that I'm probably higher ranking than him in experience, but I'll give him the benefit of the doubt this time.

"Have a seat," he motions. "You'll be working next to me handling ward one. Dr. Scully handles ward two. Dr. Preston moves between the two. We have more complex cases on this ward, and more patients at that, so your focus will be here. I'll be assigning you the cases of our previous hire. I hope you'll stick around. The patients here do get a little out of sorts at times, but I'm sure you're plenty familiar with that from where you're from. Broadmoor's reputation is unique. It's no wonder they recommended you. I've visited there once myself for a tour. Once was enough. And you were at Southside hospital before that?"

"I see you've done your research."

"Necessary after the last hire, I'm afraid. To be honest, we've had a hard time filling this position for obvious reasons. I'm sure you've seen the headlines. You also spent time in France, is that right?"

"Not long, but yes. I was in Kerhuon at a base there. Just a temporary leave, change of scenery for about eight months. France wasn't much better, but it was required of me at the time."

"And have your accommodations been sorted for you?"

"Yes, I arrived a few days ago, so I've been able to get settled in at the staff housing across the way."

"Excellent. Well, then let me show you to your office. Follow me."

He leads me out into the corridor, two doors down. "This area is quiet. It's why we put our offices here. You won't have any trouble. Patients aren't allowed down this way. This is your office."

We walk in and there are several patient files sitting on my desk already.

"You'll want to go through those. Those are the cases you'll be in charge of. You may want to pay particular attention to the Jones case, as well as the Thompson case. Dr. Preston has been filling in for me in the meantime. Mrs. Thompson and I don't bode well together. She is quite a temperamental patient. Both schizophrenia cases. Jones is rather new. Came in about four months ago. Nice enough when she's not having an episode. But her violent outbursts have become quite problematic for staff. Thompson as well. Never let her size fool you. She reverts into episodes of psychosis to avert the trauma she experienced both from her childhood and the war. I've never seen a case like it. She creates the world she can handle in her mind."

"Yes, I am aware of the Thompson case. I followed the court case closely. Quite the scandal."

"Yes, well, we have found since the incident she has been much more unpredictable. Her episodes can last days at a time. Her room has been found in a damaged state on more than one occasion. Night terrors are common. She's as crazy as her mother was. Helen Frost was a patient here as well. I remember her briefly from when I first started here. You may want to read into her case for the history. Jameson down in records can get you the file if you wish. Might help to understand Mrs. Thompson more thoroughly. She's lucid today. Might be a good time to introduce you two. Follow me."

He leads me out and down the corridor, turning left into a large room where multiple patients are sitting and eating their morning meal.

"Breakfast is at 8 a.m. All patients are expected to be here at that time or they forego their meal. No exceptions. Ah, there she is, in the corner. I've found she's not very social. Prefers to eat on her own with the exception of Kensington. She'll tolerate her on occasion. She does have a good relationship with the cook though."

"The cook?" I ask, confused.

"Yes, I can't recall his name, but Thompson will often help in the kitchen on her good days. It helps keep her focused so we allow it. Right, well I'll introduce you but before I do, I'd like to mention one last thing. I'm giving Mrs. Thompson six more months. You're quite experienced in these cases. Perhaps you know something that could help her. I've been patient for too long with her, and only because I had a good relationship with her late husband. I'm recommending her for a lobotomy if we can't find a way to help. I've been following Dr. Freeman's work for a while and I think Thompson would be a good candidate for it. But let's see what you can do, yea?"

He pats me on the shoulder as if he didn't just put the weight of the world on it and walks us over to the woman. She's naturally beautiful with auburn hair and reminds me much of my oldest daughter, Anna, who shared the same colour.

"Good morning, Ada. This is Dr. Rosco. You and him will be working together in the coming days. I wanted to introduce you two so you won't be strangers for your first therapy session. Well, I'll let you two get acquainted." Dr. Wilson rushes off, looking as if he can't wait to be rid of the people in this room.

"Ada, may I sit?"

She nods her head but doesn't say anything to me just yet. I don't blame her. I'm one more person in her life she has to learn to trust. I don't think there's many in this facility that she's been able to open up to.

"Dr. Rosco was it?"

"Yes, but you can call me Roy. Only on our one on one sessions though. Outside of that, I'm still Dr. Rosco to you."

"Are you on a first name basis with all your patients? And why are you here and not Dr. Preston?"

"I was told I might be able to help you. I like to think that I'm no better than anyone else in this room. My title doesn't dictate who I am. It's just a title. The same as widow is just a title. I do things a little differently, and I want to be able to help you for as long as I have the opportunity to do so."

"They all say that. They all want to help. If you want to help me doctor, then get me back to the man I love," she replies.

"I'm afraid I can't bring anyone back from the dead, Ada. That's a lot to ask, even of God himself. But it might help to visit your husband's grave. Sometimes closure can be found in–"

She cuts me off. "My husband was a good man, but that's not what I mean. The man I love is Kasper Bailey. I know you know the story. Everyone here does. I hear people talking, but they don't understand. I feel I'm wasting my breath even trying to tell you, the same as I've wasted it on Dr. Wilson and Dr. Preston time and time again. No one cares. No one listens. You all think you know what's best. You read through your fancy books and you run your experiments, putting us through hell because you think it will help but you're all blind, doing the same thing over and over thinking it will make medical history. If anything is crazy, it's that. You want to take the human out of the human experience just so you can pat yourselves on the back at the end of the night thinking you did a good job, when all you've done is placate us with your stupid medicines. I think we're done here, Dr. Rosco."

I'm not sure what I was expecting, but it wasn't that. There's a little prowess in that frame of hers. I can see why Dr. Wilson warned me in advance.

"Ada, please."

"Have you seen what insulin does to the body? The sweating, the salivating, the restlessness. The spasms are awful. And then your body falls into a stillness that you don't remember and they bring you back to consciousness and you're supposed to be okay but you're not. It feels like you've just been trampled on by a horse. And then you get to do it again the next day and the next day. And that's just one method they use to try and cure us. So unless you have other means to make my head right, you don't get to ask for my trust."

"All I ask is for a chance to earn it. We will be speaking again soon and I hope to change your opinion of me. Good day, Ada."

She eyes me the whole way out and when I look back, she is still staring. If looks could kill.

I introduce myself to the other staff. Nurse Arden gives me a tour of the rest of the facility, including the outside grounds.

When I finally get back to my new and much smaller office than what I'm used to, I start sorting through the patient files. Room 113 is Ms. Beverly Kensington, in here for her attempts to kill her abusive former husband. Room 118 is Mrs. Marla Lawrence, put in here by her husband for excessive masturbation and sexual desires. I set Ada's file to the side and continue to read through the patients. Samantha Bartowsky room 124: delirium. Sandra Goldstein room 132: melancholia with suicidal tendencies.

I finish up the pile, then grab the Thompson file. Something about our interaction has me feeling pulled into this case. The papers reported Ada as a victim, and since she wasn't mentally sound enough to speak for herself, the police and doctors spoke on her behalf. Attempted kidnapping, illegal sexual contact, identity fraud and assault is what they accused Jude Bailey of. It was his insistence on her mutual love that set the precedent for him to be delusional. He never stood a chance. The tabloids ate him up. Ada was a victim of her circumstances and Jude was the villain. But now that I'm here, there's more to this story and I intend to find out what exactly that is.

CHAPTER 22

Kasper

The routine of this is becoming too much to bear. No wonder men go crazy here. If they weren't before, it's only a matter of time. I'm already feeling it, and I've only been here a month. At least they let us outside. It's the only time I feel close to human.

"Listen, I'm telling you she likes me. Have you seen the way she looks over at us? Yesterday, she dropped her pen right in front of me. I picked it up for her and she thanked me!"

"No way! She thanked you?" I say sarcastically. "Archer, if you keep this up, she might fall in love with you."

"That's what I'm saying, mate. Maybe she'll put a good word in and I'll get out of here early and take her on a date. Did you and Ada ever have a date?"

I think back to our first date in the office, reminiscing on our conversations and what came after. Talking about her with Archie has been the only thing keeping me from really losing it. I need to keep her alive in my head as much as my heart.

"Yea. It was some date. But that story is just for me."

"I bet you shagged her, didn't you? I haven't been inside a woman for years. Maybe that would cure me afterall," Archie says.

"You haven't been in a woman at all, you filthy liar," says Donnie as he sits down beside him, messing up Archie's hair in the process. He really is the largest man in here, and the nurses fawn over him despite the rumours of what he did. Of course rumours have a way of running their course, but the man is nothing but a softie at heart.

"You tosser, still letting everyone think you're a wild animal even though we know the damn truth of yas," Archie responds back.

"Now, now. Leave the rumours at bay. I'd much prefer the men in here to leave us alone. Donnie has a way about him. Wouldn't want to ruin your reputation, Dons. Don't worry," I reply.

"Yea, yea. I could still take both of you at once. And then I'd steal your nurse while I was at it, Archer."

"Gentleman, sorry to interrupt but Mr. Bailey, you have a visitor."

Visits were allowed once a month only and they had to be scheduled in advance, but the men here never knew when they were coming. It was risky to get a patient wound up for a visit only to have nobody show up. The men here didn't deal well with change or disappointment. I don't know who would be visiting me. Surely it must be a mistake. The only person I care to see happens to be locked up the same as me.

I follow the nurse out of the dining hall as we head down to the visitor rooms at the front of the building. The nurse leads me to the beige room with two guards standing by the door on each side.

"Kas. It's good to see you."

"Joan. Why are you here?" I ask.

"We need to talk," she says, with a desperation in her tone.

I sit down at the chair across from her. A table in between us holds a nearly empty glass of water that she's been given.

"I didn't think this is where you'd end up. Oh Kas, how could they have done such a thing? I read all the papers and I couldn't bear to think of what your life would be like in here. Nine years is such a long time."

"I'll ask you again, Joan. Why are you here?"

She pauses, the look of guilt on her face growing heavier by the second. "I didn't think this is what would happen. I didn't think... Oh Kasper, I'm so sorry. I really didn't mean for it to come to this. I thought maybe you'd lose your job but not this."

My tone grows darker, my gaze unwavering. "What are you sorry about, Joan?"

She shakes her head, her forehead squeezing in.

I repeat myself. "What the hell are you sorry about? Speak. Now!"

"I ... I went into your flat. To see you. And I–"

"You what?!" I demand.

She looks behind her to check that the guards are still where they need to be. "I found some things and then I got curious. A work contract for Huberts? I didn't understand. So I followed you one day and you ended up at some old run down hotel. I thought it was that woman that you were meeting. I was so jealous. But when I knocked on the door after you had left, I met your friend Jimmy. He refused to talk to me at first. I showed up at his hotel the next evening and offered him money, but he refused. Some days later, he called me and I met up with him. I had to pay a pretty penny for the information but –"

I slam my fist down on the table hard, alerting the guards who both step forward. I put my hands up to them to show them I mean no harm, drawing my attention back to Joan.

"I was so mad at you. I knew I couldn't marry Theo so I ended things and then you...you were starting this whole new life just for her. So I showed up to your work one day and I saw you outside on the grounds. There was a group of you out there, but she was the only one you were looking at, and then it became clear with the way you smiled at her, and how she smiled back from a distance. You didn't see me. But I saw you. I saw who you left me for."

Ada looked beautiful that day. It was a chilly afternoon but the sun was out. Some of the women from ward one were having their outdoor leisure time and I went out to have my lunch break. I couldn't stop staring at the way her hair illuminated with the sun's rays and the way her eyes, even from a distance, glowed with golden hues of light, like they could warm me just from a single glance into them.

"A nurse that was coming in through the gates asked me if I needed help with something and I just happened to have let a few things slip."

I break out of the memory and take a deep breath to calm the racing of my heart. I can feel every vein in my head pulsing. My fists are clenched and my nostrils flare at the rage I'm currently trying to keep under control.

"You just accidentally slipped to the nurse that I wasn't who I said I was? Accidentally, Joan? You little bitch. I could strangle you right now."

"I'm sorry. I'm so sorry. And don't be mad at Jimmy. He's a good man. He was just down on his luck and well, you'll never believe this but, we're getting married! And you of all people were the one to lead me to him. The universe works in strange ways, doesn't it?"

"You need to leave. Now. No, you know what. I'm leaving!"

I get up to leave and she grabs onto my arm. "Please don't be mad. We're so sorry. We really never meant for it to get this bad."

"Oh I'm not mad. Mad does not begin to define my emotions at this moment. You vastly underestimate my fury, Joan."

"You did this to yourself, Kasper. You can blame me and Jimmy all you want, but you broke the law," she says defensively.

I laugh, the kind of laugh that prevents me from snapping Joan's neck at this very second, maniacal laughter that shows that I really should be in here.

"If it weren't for you, I'd be in France right now, living out the rest of my days with the love of my life. I don't ever want to see you or Jimmy again. Good riddance to you both." I give her one last stare, spitting at the floor beside her. "Guards, take me back upstairs."

I walk out with one of them who accompanies me upstairs.

Yes I may have broken a few laws, but it was for good reason. What they do in these facilities is not the solution, at least not for Ada. She needs love. She needs to be with someone who she can feel safe with. She needs to be with people who won't give up on her. She needs me, and I can't forgive myself for letting her down. I'll never be able to forgive myself for failing.

"Hey, there he is. So who was it?" Archie asks.

I don't say a thing to him while walking right past him to the office to find the on duty doctor.

"I want Dr. Forrester. Now," I say to the guard, preventing me from going any further to where the offices are.

"You can see him later."

Fuck this. I punch the guard square in the face, but his reflexes are faster than mine and he fights back. Another guard rushes in, followed by a third. Dr. Forrester must have heard the commotion because he comes into view while I'm being wrestled onto the floor.

"What is going on here?"

"Patient got violent in trying to find you, sir," the guard says.

"I see. Well, let's get him down to the chambers. A little confinement will help." He motions to the nurse to administer me medication. She's holding a straight jacket in her hand.

Shit.

"Two days. After that, throw him in the ice baths. After he's calmed down, then we'll talk."

I'm pulled up with my arms behind my back, a guard on each side holding my shoulders and one behind me. I see Archie's concerned face as I'm dragged out. Not the day I was planning on having, but it'll give me a story to tell Ada one day. One day.

CHAPTER 23

Ada

It's late. The moon is full tonight and a beautiful one at that. I have a perfect view of it outside my window. They call it a supermoon; at least that's what Dr. Rosco said to me today. We had our first one on one talk therapy session today. He still insists I call him Roy in our sessions, but I can't see him as anything other than a doctor at this point.

He asked me a lot of questions about Kasper and I answered them truthfully. I enjoy any excuse to talk about him. I'm sure he'll grow tired of it soon, but I'll never get tired of talking about him. I re-read all his poems today. I do every day, even the books that were destroyed. I've taken the poems out of each of those books and put them in the first book he got me, one that wasn't damaged. I hide it in the back of my wardrobe behind an old jumper so no one can find it or take it from me. It's the only physical part of him I have left.

I gaze up at the moon, wondering if Kasper can see if from where he is. The sky has a few clouds, but even then, the bright yellow of the moon beams right through the wisps that move swiftly across the top of it.

I don't know how long I stand there looking at it, mesmerized by its beauty, but I only notice that I have a visitor when I hear the door closing. I look behind me to see Nurse Arden standing there, her dark black hair casting a shadow on her face.

I don't like her and I know she doesn't like me. She glares at me each day as if her true purpose is to make my time here difficult.

"It's after hours. You need to be in bed," she says.

"I thought your shift was over. Why are you still here?"

"That's none of your concern. What is, is you being out of your bed."

I walk slowly back to my bed, hoping she'll take the hint to leave. Of course I have no intention of staying in bed. I won't waste a night like this attempting to sleep when there's a moon like that waiting for my visiting stare.

Nurse Arden gets a sinister look on her face, smiling at the satisfaction of me following her order. She then steps closer to me. "Now listen here, you little witch. If I find you out of bed again, I'll make sure your next shock therapy session lasts twice as long."

I smile back at her and let out a slight laugh. "You think you hold some kind of power here. But I see the way you bat your eyes at all the doctors. Are you that desperate for control? Do you get on your knees for them too?"

She rushes over to my bed and grabs my hair pulling me to sit up.

"You think I don't know what you did? You think I don't know what the two of you were doing in the maintenance room that night? I knew exactly what you were doing. You're nothing but a whore he used to wet his cock. He's never going to come for you and if he ever does get out, you'll be a worthless prune by then who's lost her mind, so far removed from your own reality that you won't even recognize him when he does visit. And by then, what will you look like? Not so pretty I bet. You'll both rot, slowly, painfully, until there's nothing of either of you that remains, and I'll make sure to spit on your grave when it's done."

"Why are you so angry? Did someone hurt you too?" I ask. The villain always has a backstory.

She lets go of my hair and steps back.

"I'm not angry. I'm just having a little fun."

Her face is...melting. The smile is drooping off her face as black ooze seeps out of her eyes. Startled by her appearance, I sit back further against the bed. She's terrifying. So much of her reminds me of my mother. She shares the same hair, the same sinister glare, and the same distaste for my presence. Her pupils turn white, her body as dark as her aura as she takes something out of her pocket. In her hand she holds a syringe. I don't know what's in it, but I'm not about to find out.

"You're evil. You're ... get out!" I yell.

A large spider crawls out of her mouth and sits on her shoulder, causing me to fumble out of bed. The room begins to close in on me, making me feel claustrophobic. I look up at the moon, but it's turned to coal: a large piece of hard black coal in the sky. My body is shaking as she moves closer to me.

"No!" I yell. "Get the hell away from me. Someone help!"

No one's going to come. No one ever does.

Fight back. I hear a voice from beside me. *Get her, Ada.*

I turn my head for a brief second and Edward is standing next to me. He's just the way I remember him with his short ashy brown hair, grey eyes and round spectacles around them. His face is pale and his body nearly translucent with his favorite brown striped suit he always wore with his matching fedora.

I look away for a split second back at the nurse and when I return once more to look at Edward, he's gone.

Nurse Arden moves towards me threateningly. I grab the small lamp from my side table and turn toward her, smashing the shade over her head. She falls back, dropping the needle but not hard enough for it to break the glass vile. I go to reach for it but she wraps her arms around my throat and pulls me back into her, cutting off my air supply. I throw my head back, knocking it into her face which causes her to release me. It gives me enough time to hold the upper hand as I turn around and straddle her, slapping her hard in the face, stunning her as I reach for the uncapped needle. She attempts to reach for it too, but I grab it just before her from the floor, turn back to her and puncture it into her chest, pushing the medicine into her. I have no idea what it is, but she looks shocked for a moment until her body relaxes and her head collapses to the floor.

She's back in her normal form now, and when I look up, Dr. Rosco is standing there. I drop the needle to my side and shuffle myself back against the wall, tears silently falling down my face.

"That woman is a demon," I release.

"What did you give her, Ada?" He asks.

"Whatever she was trying to give me."

He just nods, seeing the damaged lamp on the floor and the blood coming from the side of Nurse Arden's head. He runs into the hall to get the attention of a couple staff members, then comes to my side and crouches down.

"Okay. Let's get you back into bed."

I comply, crawling into bed, wrapping my arms around my knees under the blanket tightly, while Dr. Rosco sees to the nurse.

Someone else enters the room, but I'm too preoccupied to notice who it is because I'm looking once again at Edward, who is standing beside my bed looking down on me. His face is expressionless. I tighten the grip around my knees and stare at him in fright. My breath quickens as my heart beat races from the remaining adrenaline. I get out on the other side of the bed and run out of the room, needing an escape. I need to get out of here. I need to get away from all of this. I'm almost at the stairwell when the guard on duty grabs me.

"Come on, Ada. Not again. Go back to bed."

I start walking with him back to my room, knowing I've blown any chance of getting away tonight.

"I don't want to go back in there," I say to Dr. Rosco, who's met me and the guard in the hall.

"Let's talk about this in the morning. You need sleep. You know very well what happens when you don't sleep."

"I'm not tired. Please, can I go to the lounge room for a little bit? I don't want to go back in there. Please. I can't see him. I can't, just please."

"See who?" he asks.

"Edward. He knows. He's mad at me for falling in love with Kasper. I know it."

Dr. Rosco sighs. "I'm going to go with you into the lounge room. You get one hour to cool down, and then you need to go back to bed. Understand?"

"Yes, thank you!" A sense of relief washes over me. "Why are you here at this hour anyway? I thought you would have gone home by now."

"I've got much on my mind. There were some things I needed to finish up."

He walks with me and the guard down to the lounge room. I hear him telling the guard to stay close. He sits in a rusty brown coloured chair in the corner of the room, and I go to the couch, letting my legs run long ways across it. I can still see the moon from here from a window overlooking the courtyard. I notice there's a small hole in the wall beside the window. It's next to the corner of a picture that has no glass. The hole looks like a spider, with little scribbly cracks coming out of it that look like legs. I don't like it. I get up and walk over to it and tilt the picture slightly to cover it before going back to the couch to resume my previous position.

"Hey, Roy. Do you think you could come with me to visit my father's grave tomorrow? I haven't been to it this week and I think it would be good to go see him."

"Your father's grave?"

"Yes, it could use some new flowers. Do you have any dried flowers? He never liked things to die on his account, so he only had dried flowers in the house after my mother was put away."

Roy straightens up. "Ada, who am I to you?"

"Roy, don't be so silly. You're my friend. Someone who works at the same hospital Kasper used to work at. Do you think they'll find him for me? I miss him. I miss him so much. Did you ever love someone like that?"

He breathes heavily. "I did, yes."

"What was her name?"

He stalls before answering, chewing on his lip. "Ivy."

"How come I've never heard about her before? Tell me about her," I say to him while I fixate on the bright ball of light out my window.

"She was my first and only love. I met her at a ballroom dance in 1920. She was the only woman that would dance with me that night. It was an instant kind of love. I knew the second I held her hand that she was the one. We married only six months later, against our parents wishes. We had two children, two girls. Anna and Everly. We had a good life."

"Had?" I question.

He clears his throat. "There was an accident in 1945. It was a train derailment. My daughters were on it. Anna and her soon to be husband had gone to visit his family. I didn't like the guy much. Perhaps it was because he reminded me so much of my younger self. Everly went with her as a chaperone, but they never arrived. I was so hard on Anna in the days before, trying to convince her that she was making a mistake with him. Ivy had a hard time with the deaths. We all did. But a mother should never have to bury her own children. It was too painful for her and she took her own last year."

I'm nearly in tears at his story, my heart empathetically hurting along with his. I walk over to him and crouch down in front of him, holding his hand in mine. "Roy, why didn't you tell me? I'm so sorry! I can't imagine losing my –" That strange feeling is back.

"I'm okay, Ada. Thank you for being a good friend. It's not something I talk about often. I really think you should get some sleep now. I can come visit you tomorrow and we can talk some more. I'm quite tired myself."

Of course, how selfish of me. It's late for him. I shouldn't have kept him so late. "Yes, of course. Let me walk you out."

After Roy leaves, I head back to my room. I get into bed and close my eyes, feeling the residual grief from Roy's story. I notice the book that Kasper gave me with the pages of poems, sitting on my nightstand. I could have sworn I had put them back in the wardrobe. Either way, I open the book and take out the last one he left me, one he hid under my pillow the week before everything fell apart. I read it over and over again until I drift off to sleep.

SUPPLE IS YOUR FLESH THAT SUMMONS MY TEETH.

YOUR SCARS AND MINE, OUR LOVE BEQUEATH.

Our sins of past we leave to decay.
I will come for you before I stray.
And if by chance they confine me,
I'll fight for you until I'm free.

Your Kasper

CHAPTER 24

Roy

Today is my day off and I'm heading out of town on what you could call a little work road trip. Though it's unconventional, I need as much information as I can get to help my patient. I've got five months remaining until Dr. Wilson ruins all chances of Ada having any semblance of reality. I don't agree with his methods; archaic and repugnant like most doctors of a certain age who can't seem to look beyond the basic literature and into their own humanity.

I pull into Stanfield and wait for a guard to open the front gates for me after taking my name.

After I park my car and walk to the front of the building, I see a crowd of people gathered around one of the larger set of windows upstairs. They watch my every move, curious to any outsider that breaches their territory. I'm let in through the large front doors.

"Good afternoon, sir. How may I help you?" a woman greets me.

"Good afternoon. I'm here to see one of your patients, a Mr. Bailey, that is."

A familiar man walks over to join in on the conversation. "Dr. Rosco, it's good to see you," Dr. Forrester greets me, shaking my hand.

Dr. Forrester and I have been acquainted before and luckily for my benefit, he happens to be the head doctor at this facility.

He continues. "We will have two guards on duty in the room with you. I would caution you to speak respectfully to Mr. Bailey. He is not a forgiving man and is easily triggered. I do look forward to hearing about your meeting. Some of the cases here present with more difficulty than others, Mr. Bailey being one of them. He is getting out of his second round of confinement. A stubborn one he is. Follow me."

He leads me down the hall into a white room with a window facing to the front grounds of the property with an overgrown bush covering the bottom portion of the window pane. There's a small table in the middle where I sit down.

"Can I get you a glass of water while you wait? We don't tell the inmates in advance of visitors. Some may think it's better to prepare them, but we prefer to prevent the build up of anticipation."

"No water for me, thank you," I reply.

"Very well. I'll leave you to it."

I wait about fifteen minutes or so until the guards come to the door, patient and part prisoner in tow.

Kasper is a tall man with messy dark blond hair and a look on his face that screams trouble. He has a small cut above his right eye and a bruise yellowing on his jaw.

I stand up to greet my visiting patient, offering my hand out to him. "Mr. Bailey, I'm Doctor Rosco, but you can call me Roy. Nice to finally meet you."

He stares down at me suspiciously, refusing to shake my hand. *Fair enough.* Sitting down in front of me, he leans back in his chair and looks around the room as if reliving a moment.

"I'm going to get right to the point. I'm here with good intentions and that's to help my patient, a patient I believe you to be quite familiar with. Ada Thompson."

That immediately snaps his attention back to me, straightening his stature in the chair.

"You've seen Ada? Is she okay? Does she know where I am?"

"I'm going to get to everything, but I need you to remain calm while we discuss this. I know it's a sensitive topic and I'm here to help."

He nods his head in understanding, but his breathing is rapid and he's fiddling one hand with the other anxiously.

"Ada is okay. She's in my care for the time being, though Dr. Wilson is still overseeing the case at large."

"Scoundrel," he mumbles under his breath.

"She speaks of you often, even when she's having her episodes. She seems to change her reality and everyone in it, but yet you remain constant regardless of what state she is in. However, she doesn't always seem to align the ending of your story about you leaving. She is always asking where you are and when she'll see you. What I'm going to share with you next is confidential patient information and I'm going to ask you to respect that privacy."

Kasper nods his head impatiently in agreement wanting all the information I can give him.

I lean my arms forward on the table and lower my voice just slightly. "To be honest, from what I've read in her file, her condition has gotten worse since your last encounter on the day you were arrested. She's made multiple attempts to escape. She's in and out of lucidity. She's become violent on more than one occasion with one of the nurses. She's also isolated herself from the group during recreational time. But if there's one thing I've learned about Ada over the last month, it's that she truly loves you and that's why I want to help. Think of it as another experiment. The reports I read from when you were unlawfully employed at the institution show Ada being in not only good health, eating, sleeping better, but her behaviour and symptoms improved. I'd like to see what we can do with that by reintroducing you to her. I don't want to give either of you a sense of false hope, but more so a small bridge of communication to see if it will help her case."

He leans in on the table, his eyes wide and moving between mine. "I'll take a bridge, any bridge. Just tell me what I need to do."

I pull out a piece of paper and a pen from my jacket pocket.

"She knows your writing style I assume from the poems she reads. You wrote those?"

"Every one of them."

I nod in appreciation. "Write to her. I'll make sure she gets it. If it goes well, I'll visit again."

"A bridge," he repeats, nodding back. "Okay."

I hand him the piece of paper and pen. He holds the pen in his hand for a minute adjusting the paper, looking up at me first and then staring at the white sheet while he figures out what to write. It takes him about ten minutes to write the letter and I don't say a single word to him while he is concentrating on it. He re-reads it, folds it in half, then hands me the paper.

"I'm not a trusting man, doc. Don't you hurt her. I won't be in here forever," he says as a warning.

"I'll be in touch," I say, getting up.

He stays seated as I walk out. A member of staff is waiting for me nearby.

"I'll take you to Dr. Forrester's office. Right this way," the woman leads.

I fill the doctor in on the details of our visit, having full support in the matter.

Dr. Wilson might not entirely approve of my approach, but I plan to make sure he doesn't involve himself in this case as much as possible and prove him wrong. I take out the letter, tempted to read it, but even I respect the privacy of a fellow man.

Kasper looks like he's seen better days and perhaps, just maybe, better days are ahead.

CHAPTER 25

Ada

I woke up today and wanted to die. My head is pounding and I think I'm running a temperature. Looney Loo takes a seat next to me at supper when the last thing I want to hear is her gossip.

"Hello, Silvia," I greet her.

"Hello there, hun. How's the day for ya? I bet all that rain will break free soon and we can get out to get some air, let the spirits out for a breather. All this energy in here is getting to me. Ya hear about the woman on the second ward? Apparently she started talking in a new voice with a Scots accent of all things. She's from London, so you can understand the surprise. Nurse said she had a new name but the same body. I overheard them talking. I bet it's one of them spirits takin' hold. They do that, ya know. I wouldn't be surprised if they came after one of us. Over my dead body, I tell yas. They won't get to me."

"Maybe you won't know it if they do. I bet the woman doesn't remember a thing. They could be watching you right now, waiting until you sleep to invade you," I jokingly reply.

"Now don't yous go on like that. That kind of talk is good for no one around here. Not even for you. I heard you tried to kill Nurse Arden. Darla told me she heard yous screaming and that Nurse Arden got carried out. I wouldn't want to get on the wrong side of you. Maybe those spirits have gotten to you already."

"Good evening ladies, I'm wondering if I can borrow Mrs. Thompson. I have a matter to discuss."

I'm grateful for the excuse to leave. I follow Dr. Rosco to his office and take the familiar chair. It's strange being in here. Kasper and I have memories of this room and each time I come in here, it carries me back in time. I'm starting to wonder if I'll ever see him again.

The doctor hands me a piece of paper without explanation. I take a glance at him in question, then open the folded note and suck in a quick breath.

"Read it first," he gestures at the letter.

It's *his* writing. It really is. I know it by now the way I know the palm of my hand.

Peach,

I don't have a lot of time to write this and I know this is going to come as a surprise. I'm sorry. I'm sorry that we didn't get to leave. I'm sorry it ended up like this. I wake up each morning with the guilt heavy on my shoulders and the thoughts of you that never cease during the day. And at night, I add to them, bringing you to life if only until I drift into sleep. I'm getting out of here some day and you'll be the first person I come to find when I do. Don't give up hope, pretty girl. Our story isn't done yet.

Yours only,
Kasper

"He didn't give up." I say to myself. "He really wrote this! How did you make this happen?"

"I have some connections. There's an old colleague there that I worked with for a bit at Broadmoor before he took over at Stanfield. I'm going to need you to keep this quiet, Ada. For now at least. I'll schedule another visit at the end of the month. You can think about what you'd like to write him back. But in the meantime, no sedating any nurses. I've moved Nurse Arden to the second ward for now. She's a trigger for you."

"She's a vile bitch who –"

He cuts me off. "You don't need to finish that sentence."

"Oh but I do! She's out to get me. You don't understand. She's snuck into my room before. I know it! She's the only one that could have wrecked my books. Just last week, I came back from the supper hall and all my things were on the floor. She tried to blame me, but it's her, I swear. I know your job is to discern all the stories you get from your patients. But nobody ever believes us here. They label us crazy and any of the truths we came with get left behind the second we step foot in here."

"I'm not here to judge you. I don't believe Nurse Arden had your best interest and that's why I had her moved. You and her have a problematic history and Dr. Wilson and I agreed."

"It was Dr. Wilson that let her back here to begin with. She was already sent over to the second ward when Kasper was here. Can't you fire her?"

"No, that's not within my control. But rest assured, she won't be coming near you while I'm here."

I want to believe him. And maybe giving me this letter is a small sign of his trust, but I've been here long enough to know how this works. People don't give you something without taking something in return. Most of the time, it's our dignity.

"Thank you for the letter. May I go now?"

"Yes, and remember what I said. Keep it quiet."

"I will," I assure him.

Both of us walk into the hall only to be greeted by Dr. Wilson. I slip the letter into my dress pocket before he notices.

"Ah, Ada. I believe Ms. Kensington was looking for you. She would like some assistance in planning the Christmas dance this year. I told her I'm sure you'd be happy to help in the planning."

This is the second year he's volunteered me for this task. I didn't enjoy myself much last year and I doubt I'll have any fun this time around, but Beverly and I seem to get along and lucky for them both, I'm in a good mood thanks to Dr. Rosco's surprise.

"Yes, I'll go find her. Thank you Doctor."

"She's in a good mood today," I hear Dr. Wilson say, as I walk away.

Beverly is in the rec room with a large drawing of the main dining hall that we turn into our celebratory room for Christmas. It's a day everyone looks forward to all year. Christmas is still a couple months away, but the planning always begins in the fall. Mainly I think it's so we won't get bored and instead, occupy ourselves with something to keep up morale. It's the one day of the year we're served a large feast with proper desserts.

"Ada, so glad you can help again this year. Let's get to it then."

I sit down across from Beverly. We start to discuss decorations and where we would like the main tree to go. We hand make all the decorations ourselves each year and though we always save some for the following year, there's more to be added or repaired.

Dr. Wilson comes in to collect a fellow patient for their therapy session and Beverly looks over at him with a dark stare.

"Something the matter?" I ask.

"Sure there is while he's still here. Poor ol' Marcy was nearly frozen to death. You know how she gets all hyped up sometimes. Dr. Wilson put her in an ice bath. Or at least he ordered it. Nurses were instructed to keep her in there for a certain time, but she was in there too long. Nearly died, she was so cold. I heard he's shagging a couple of the nurses here too. An old man like him, thinking he's got power over the women here. I don't know how he even gets it up at his age. The sad thing is, they're tame here compared to other facilities. Did you know that Dr. Rosco used to work at Broadmoor? I hear they torture the patients there. The worst of the worst are kept there. Men that have done terrible things, worse than anyone kept here. I bet Dr. Rosco's been a part of that work. I just hope he doesn't bring it here."

"For some reason, I don't think he's like that. Maybe that's why he's here, to get away from all that. He seems kind. I think we ought to give him the benefit of the doubt. I'll take him over Dr. Wilson any day of the week," I reply.

"You might be right. I guess we're sure to see."

CHAPTER 26

Kasper

It's been three weeks since Dr. Rosco last visited and I'm becoming more anxious by the day. Donnie and I sit at the same table we do for breakfast each day, discussing matters of our escape plan. We decided to let another guy in on our talks. Sheldon is his name. He was brought in for something called manic depression. Donnie says we can trust him so we're giving him a chance. He's the smallest out of the four of us and looks even smaller sitting next to Donnie.

"I usually get a visit from my brother on the last Saturday of the month. He can help," Sheldon says.

"Isn't your brother the reason you're in here?" I ask.

"Well yes, but it's not his fault. I stole his car and gambled away his money. I don't blame him. He could have pummeled my arse but he didn't. I deserved it too. I don't have any intentions to leave this place. My brother would bring me right back here, but I'll get you two buggers out of here at least. Where's Archer anyway? He's supposed to be here."

I look around the room and notice Archie is nowhere to be seen. He's my bedmate but wasn't there this morning when I woke up.

"Probably took him down for treatment," Donnie suggests.

"I'll go have a look," I say, getting up from the table.

"Where do you think you're going?" One of the guards at the door asks.

"Lavatory. Porridge is running right through me."

He moves aside and I walk down the long corridor, keeping an eye out for Archie but I don't see him anywhere. There's a *cleaning in progress* sign on the door, but I don't let it deter me from checking anyway. I pop my head in for a second and hear the low moans of a man. Being deprived of a woman for so long here can make one desperate for touch. It's not an uncommon thing to listen to the men wank off in their beds while we are trying to sleep. Some of them wait until shower day to do their business.

I'm just about to leave when I hear a desperate cry, "Please. Stop!"

I know that voice. I kick open the door, round the corner and see Archie pushed over the counter, blood running down his face, tears watering down the red and a guard standing behind him with their pants down. Archie looks at me, shame in his expression with a plea to help in his eyes. I don't stop to think a second longer. I impulsively lunge toward the guard, knocking him down to the ground, his pants still down around his ankles as Archie moves back towards the door. I don't know where he disappears to. The only thing now in my vision is the guard whose face I'm bloodying.

"You fucking bastard!" I yell at him. *Punch!* I lift his shoulders up off the ground then slam him back down. *Punch!*

His nose is bloody, his face trying to make sense of the assault he's living through but I don't relent. I punch him over and over again until his face is a bloody mess and I'm being pulled off by two other guards.

"You're all bastards!" I yell. "Forcing yourselves on already weak men."

I'm dragged out of the room, a baton hitting the side of my face and I black out.

When I wake up, I'm back in solitary confinement. Third times a charm. I wonder how long they will put me in for this time. The first time it was a couple days. The Second visit, five days. I might as well be in prison.

It's dark in the room, light only peaking through the tiny barred window facing another wall. You think men are crazy when they come in, but they are even crazier after spending days in a room like this. However, there's perspective to be found in this situation. Getting out of this room feels like an illusion of freedom moving back into the other quarters. There's no justice in this place, not when you have guards who don't know how to control their own urgencies.

I don't know how long I was knocked out for. I haven't seen a single soul since I've woken up.

I change my position on the squeaky frame of the thin mattress, turning on the side opposite of where my head was hit. I've got a pounding headache and my fist is covered in dried blood, blue and purple marking the area around it. I squeeze my hand in and out trying to stretch my fingers only to feel shooting pain down through my knuckles.

Worth it.

***

3 Days Later

There's a double knock at the metal cell door. "Bailey. You've got a visitor."

Pretty sure they don't let those of us in here have visitors, but it must be Dr. Rosco because he's the only one who would have any pull.

The door opens and the light bursts in, my sensitive eyes needing time to adjust. My head is still hurting and my hand still swollen, though relatively better than what it was.

"Let's go. No funny business or the jacket goes on," the guard threatens, motioning me out of the cell. When I move into the hall, there are two other guards opposite of him waiting for me. I'm walked back to the visitor area, God knows looking worse for wear. I haven't showered since before the incident so I'm sure I stink, having been stuck in this room for all this time with the same clothes.

When I walk into the room, I see Dr. Rosco sitting down at the table, his eyes widening at my appearance.

"Don't try anything or we'll drag your arse right back in there, d'ya hear?"

I don't say anything but sit down at the small table across from the doctor feeling defeated.

"You look like shite," Dr. Rosco says.

"Thanks, Doc. Hard work being a hero around here."

"You beat a guard to a bloody pulp," he reminds me.

"He deserved it. I'd do the same for you if you were being defiled by one of these wankers."

He's caught off guard for a second and the men standing at the door look down uncomfortably, knowing the truth of what really transpired.

"If you want me to help you, you can't be getting yourself into trouble."

"How do you plan on helping me exactly? Helping Ada is one thing, but I've got no shot in hell to leave here with any other authority than my own."

"What's that supposed to mean?" he inquires.

"Nothing," I look down in response.

I can see him in my peripheral vision trying to figure me out. He doesn't say anything further, but instead slides an envelope my way. I grab it quickly, opening it up with anticipation to see Ada's handwriting on it.

Kasper

Tell me, my love. When you look at the moon, when you see the stars, do you think of me? I can't tell you what it means to hear your voice, if only through words. This place has a hold on me when the only one I want to hold me is you. I'm nothing but a phantom roaming the halls in limbo waiting to see you again. You've given me something so few get to have in this life, and that's rare unconditional love that moves beyond these walls. I hope you can feel it there. I hope you can still feel me. The only thing you should ever be sorry about, is not finding me sooner. I wish we had more time, but even if our bodies wither, even if our souls escape, we will find each other.

All my love,
Ada

I don't just read it once, I read it three times. The doctor snaps me out of my momentary escape, handing me a fresh piece of paper and a pen. I grab it right away, tucking the existing letter into my pocket and start writing.

Once I'm done, I fold the piece of paper in half, handing it to him once again, in hopes that he'll follow through and give it to her.

"Don't tell her about what happened. I don't want her to worry. I don't want this to be the picture in her head she sees of me."

"I won't," he assures me. "I've got four more months on her case. I'm going to be scheduling visits every fortnight from here on out. Dr. Forrester is aware. However, if you should find yourself in solitary again, these visits will be postponed, and I will not be able to promise you that bridge."

"I understand."

"Good. Bye for now, Mr. Bailey." He gets up, puts on his hat and walks out of the room.

Dr. Forrester walks in nodding to Dr. Rosco in passing. "I was going to give you a week this time, but under the circumstances, I think three days will be sufficient. Unless you think we should escort you back to solitary?"

"No sir, I think three days has been plenty."

"Right. Well, then let's go. But should you end up assaulting another guard, it'll be two weeks. Do you understand?"

"Yes, I understand," I reply, squeezing my fists while standing up next to the other guards.

"And Mr. Bailey, before you go. I should tell you that the guard you assaulted has been let go from duty, so you shouldn't be seeing him again."

He walks out before I respond, as a warning to the other guards who take me back up to the men's quarters.

It looks to be just after the lunch hour, my eyes still adjusting from the sun beaming in through the larger windows. I walk into the dining hall and Donnie stands up first, coming over to greet me.

"Thought we might not see you again. We have some catching up to do." He sniffs. "On second thought, you're rank. Don't you dare sit your arse down with us until you've had a proper clean."

I laugh in response. "Good to see you too, Donnie."

Archie is over at the table with his head down but notices me and nods with no smile on his face, no words, no intention of coming to see me. It's a silent understanding of his gratitude. My three days were nothing compared to his suffering and if I had to go back and do it again, I would gladly accept two more weeks. But now I need to keep my head clear. I owe it to Ada to see this through. If I can't help myself, I can at least try and help her.

CHAPTER 27

Roy

Tick, tick, tick. I stare at my clock that sounds louder today than usual. I have three months left before Dr. Wilson decides Ada's fate. And not only Ada but Jones as well, two of Wilson's toughest cases that he's gotten lazy on.

Ada hasn't fallen into any major episodes since the first letter, aside from some things she's mentioned that she sees in her room at night. I'm starting to wonder if a change in environment would help her to sleep better. To be in the same institution that your own mother died in seems to be a cruel form of punishment. These walls have seen their fair share of pain, and who knows what ghosts will haunt this place in the years to come.

I've delivered two more letters to Kasper and Ada in the past month, having just finished our last visit a couple days back. Dr. Forrester has said that there have been no further issues with Kasper since his last stay in confinement. It looks like both Ada and Kasper are doing better since making contact.

I have an idea that I'll need approval for in order to make happen. Dr. Forrester and I were discussing the upcoming holiday season in hopes of trying to bring up the morale in the facilities, but how to go about it in a safe manner will be another matter altogether. I'll have to come clean with Dr. Wilson if I'm going to have any chance of this working.

I knock lightly on Dr. Wilson's door but don't hear a response. I open it slightly, knocking again while doing so and startle him with my presence. Nurse Arden stands up from the floor and wipes her mouth and Dr. Wilson immediately fiddles with his trousers. I'm not supposed to see this but given the gossip from other staff members, I'm also not surprised. I close the door immediately and wait outside of it. I can hear from the door that they are arguing, or more so, that Dr. Wilson is raising his voice. Nurse Arden opens the door with her head down and walks away.

This is exactly what I need. Leverage.

He clears his throat, "Come in Rosco."

Still using my name informally. *Prick.*

"A little courtesy would do you some good. Now what was so important that you needed to interrupt me?"

"May I sit?" I ask, skipping over the awkwardness of his earlier words.

"Yes, yes. I have to be somewhere so make it quick."

"Well, as you know we've had some improvements in Mrs. Thompson's case. We've once again stopped the traditional therapies. The Metrazol was proving to be more problematic for her. We're focusing more on one on one psychotherapy now. She's had more lucid days lately. Aside from some mild hallucinations brought on when she is fatigued, her symptoms have greatly improved over the last month. I have been using an unconventional approach, which I feel is benefitting Mrs. Thompson and that is by having her exchange correspondence with Mr. Bailey. I've been working closely with Dr. Forrester at Standfield and he agrees Mr. Bailey has also been more cooperative."

“Exchanging correspondence? Rosco, you are walking a dangerous line. The two of them will only make it worse for each other down the road. You don’t know what you’re doing.”

“I disagree. Both her condition during Mr. Bailey’s unlawful employment here as well as what I’m seeing now is indication that their connection is only improving their outcome. I’d like to take this further by reintroducing them in person. It’s a fair experiment to see if Ada’s condition remains stable, or if she reverts back into psychosis; a trigger or a solution.”

Dr. Wilson shakes his head. “You’ve gone too far on this one Rosco. I deem this highly inappropriate.”

“Doctor, if your wife was taken from you and put into an institution similar to the very one we’re in right now, with no chance to make contact, how would you fare?”

“That’s not the same situation. He’s a criminal and a lunatic.”

“He’s a man in love,” I correct him. “Would you not go crazy if you had been separated from the woman you wanted to spend your life with?”

“You know, they might be doing me a favour. I hardly see my wife as is even now. She has her life. I have mine.”

I’m frustrated by his response but expect it at the same time. Of course he doesn’t love his wife. He was just getting his cock sucked by one of the nurses. I wouldn’t be surprised if he and his wife share separate homes.

“I’m proposing that we have the Christmas Ball in Stanfield. They have a bigger hall, more secure facilities, more on duty guards. Dr. Forrester and I discussed having a lottery. We have only 78 active patients, they have over triple that. Transferring from their hospital would be more difficult given their cases. They have about 14% self admitting cases and we have 25%. It just makes sense to have it there versus here. If we run a lottery giving 100 spots out for the ball, that would bring our numbers to a little over 200 with staff. It would not only boost morale for both facilities, but men love to compete. A lottery would be the best bet. Stanfield doesn't normally have celebrations so this would be a fair opportunity and most of those men haven't had any interaction with the opposite sex in quite some time. We'd make sure Mr. Bailey and Mrs. Thompson would be among them of course, with guards at all exits."

"These patients must be getting to you, Rosco, because you're out of your mind if you think we're going to transfer 78 of our patients to a facility nearly two hours away for a ball." He laughs and shakes his head, turning his attention away from me to a folder that's sitting on his desk of new admittances.

"It's *Dr.* Rosco and I think the supportive evidence would be in my favour if I bring this to the board, which I will do if necessary. It would very much benefit both facilities' reputations in the public eye. All they need is your stamp of approval otherwise. You oversee the majority of this facility and that doesn't go unnoticed, but you hired me for a reason and it would be a shame to let a woman like Ada Thompson fall through the cracks because I didn't try everything. We have a limited timeline to make this come together. I will keep your private activities with Nurse Arden to myself, and in turn, you will approve this."

I smile at him knowing very well the penalty that would be consequential to him if his indulgences were to be made public. He stares at me with a grimace and cracks his knuckles.

"If this little experiment of yours goes wrong, you will not only be held responsible, but I will move forward with Ada's plan sooner than expected. You have a lot to lose here, Rosco. I look forward to seeing your failure."

I hate this man.

I leave the office without another word and call Dr. Forrester to discuss the plans for the event. Then I look for Ms. Kensington.

"Ah, Beverly. I'd like to discuss with you a few things for the upcoming Christmas Ball. You and Ada have been collaborating on this?"

"Yes doctor, Ada and I are creating some really great new decorations for this year. I think it will be even better than last year."

"That's wonderful, but there has been an update for this year's plans that I should mention. Instead of an evening event, we'll be having one mid day and the location has changed. We'll be moving it to another facility with a larger space."

"But sir, we've already organized the whole layout. There's only four weeks until the day. How are we going to make all the changes with such little time?"

"Not to worry. I'd like for you and Ada to gather six others to help you with the set up. I'll have plans drawn up for you of the new room. The tree will be delivered there instead. I'll take care of that as well as the transportation. Stanfield will sort out the food and refreshments with the exception of desserts that we will be in charge of. All good fun I think."

"Stanfield? Sir?"

"Yes, Beverly," I confirm.

"Oh, wait till Ada hears of this. It'll knock the knickers right off her you know!"

I smile, knowing I'm taking part in this little love story. I just have to hope it has a happy ending.

CHAPTER 28

Kasper

Each night that I fall asleep to Ada's letters, it's a reminder that if I don't wake up, I will have had at least this. The morning comes too soon and I'm pulled out of my dreams of her into the reality I've been cursed in.

Archie hasn't been here for the last two days, but he showed up this morning for breakfast with a smile on his face and in good spirits.

"Where have you been?" I ask.

"Just having treatment. Doctor kept me for observation."

"What kind of treatment?" I push.

Before I can get the answer, I hear Dr. Forrester trying to quiet everyone down.

"Gentleman, if I can have your attention."

The hall gradually quiets, a few whispers still being heard throughout.

"Christmas is just weeks away. Each year, we have a Christmas dinner in the hall, which will go on as scheduled this year on December 25th. However, we have invited some friends to join us for a Christmas Ball on December 24th to celebrate the holiday with a little more joy this year."

Cheers erupt in the hall but the doctor puts up his hand to silence everyone once again.

"However. Due to the numbers, there will only be allotted one hundred of you for the ball."

Once again, noise breaks out and complaints follow. The doctor continues trying to speak over the protests.

"There will be a lottery held to choose who will attend and any disruptions in behaviour will disqualify one from being entered into the lottery. The names will be chosen in two weeks time. Those who wish not to attend may give their place to someone else. That is all."

Donnie speaks first. "I wonder who they're inviting. Maybe some lassies. We've got too many men here. Could use some change."

"I don't care about that any more. But maybe I'll get some mistletoe for Nurse Barker and I. Sneak a little smooch from her for my Christmas present. I've been a good boy this year after all," Archie says, winking.

"That may be for you Archer, but Kas here's only getting coal. Doubt you'll even be entered into the lottery," Donnie teases me.

"Now, now, he's been good lately ever since getting those letters from his woman. How about that now. She's going to be awfully jealous if you end up at the ball with the ladies," Archie says.

"I have no interest in attending any ball. One of you can take my place if I get called," I say, looking around the room at all the men in their excitement. "Besides, balls are for the pretentious elite. What kind of ball do you think we'll have here in a fucking loonie bin of all places? All we've got is our day clothes. Are they going to give us suits to wear? Tuxedos perhaps? Will we be drinking sparkling wine and being served hors-d'oeuvres? Get your heads out of the gutters. This is nothing but a stunt to make Stanfield look good from all the rumours going about. A marketing stunt is all."

"Bah humbug. Where's your Christmas spirit?" Archer asks.

"Mr. Bailey," Dr. Forrester calls my attention. "You have a visitor. Please come with me."

"Yes, sir." I comply knowing that the good doc is waiting for me, hopefully to give me another letter.

"I'll be sitting in on the visit today."

Curiosity ruminates through me. Why would Dr. Forrester need to witness my meeting with doc Roy?

We're let out of the solid locked doors and head down the stairs to the first floor, towards the front of the building where Dr. Rosco is waiting for us in the same room as all the times before. He stands up to greet me and I nod my head, taking the seat across from him as Dr. Forrester takes the seat next to him. Dr. Rosco holds the letter from Ada in his hand but he doesn't give it to me just yet. He places it on the table in front of him lining it up on the edge.

Dr. Forrester begins. "I'm pleased to say that your behavior and therapy sessions have been going well. You've managed to keep your head straight enough not to end up back in confinement. With that said, what we're about to tell you is to remain a private matter. Should this information get out to any further patients or staff for that matter, we will cancel the event."

More questions are stirring through me but I let him continue without interruption.

"The ball that will take place on December 24th will be with the residents of Huberts Home. You are familiar with them and of one patient in particular I believe."

My heart starts pounding and I feel a cold sensation run through my body at the news but still, I stay quiet. This is too good to be true. There's always a catch.

"Mrs. Thompson will be in attendance. She's tasked to help set up for the event with a small group of women."

"Don't call her Mrs. Thompson. It's "Ms.," I correct him. "Her husband is no longer here nor there, and the only way she'll be called Mrs. is when she is Mrs. Bailey."

Dr. Forrester's eyes zone in on me whereas Dr. Rosco looks down.

"It is of course correct to call her Mrs. having been widowed, Mr. Bailey."

"Ada and I don't follow the rules, Doctor Forrester, if you haven't already realized."

"Careful Kasper. We're giving you an opportunity here," Dr. Rosco warns.

I check myself knowing he's right. I won't let a dead man ruin my mood. My Ada is coming here, and I need to do whatever I can to see her. It might be the only opportunity I have to finally get away with her.

"You will be on your very best behavior, Mr. Bailey. There will be eyes on you at all time. Do not do anything that will compromise this experiment. If you do, the letters between you will stop and we will cease all contact with *Ms.* Thompson," Dr. Forrester warns.

A bridge. I need this bridge.

"Do you understand what we are saying, Mr. Bailey?" Dr. Forrester asks.

"I do, sir. I assure you that I will not take this opportunity for granted."

"Good. Well, I'll leave you two to finish up. Dr. Rosco, pleasure as always."

The two doctors exchange handshakes and when Dr. Forrester leaves the room, Dr. Rosco pulls his attention back to me. He doesn't say anything for a moment. He watches me while I eye the letter, and when I look at him to meet his stare, he further observes me, an awkwardness brewing in the room as the seconds pass. After a minute, he finally speaks.

"What are you planning?"

"I don't know what you're talking about," I defend while shifting in my chair.

"Cut the nonsense. I can see it congregating inside your head."

I look away, breaking eye contact. He's right of course. I'm planning every possible exit in my head, every distraction I can use. My plan to get out of here has been moving, but slow. Sheldon met with his brother and passed him a letter of the things we would need. Sneaking that in front of the guards wasn't an easy task and his brother was reluctant to even consider the idea, even with a monetary deal to back it up. Trying to get the supplies into this place would be another challenge in itself. All I have is time and though I want to be impatient, this has got to be done right. But with only weeks away till Christmas Eve, a plan B might have to come into place.

"I want to help you. But you're going to have to trust me and I know that's not an easy thing for you to do. I know you've been let down by just about everyone in your life. I know you're in here because a friend outed you. I know you have very little reason to trust me, but I need you to anyway. If you try to run, Kasper, whether it be today or at the ball, or any other day you have planned, I will be forced to not only burn our bridge, but I will lose my position. It also means losing any contact with Ada. It's not only your life at stake here, Kasper. It's now mine too and hers."

I continue my silence. He waits for me to respond, but I'm letting the possibilities run through my head a million miles a second.

He sighs like he's holding back on me. I can see the evidence of stress burrowing its way onto his forehead.

"Kasper, Dr. Wilson is pushing for a lobotomy for Ada. If this fails, she will no longer be my patient and she will no longer be Ada."

My veins turn to ice and I'm staring at the doctor with a pain in my eyes I know he can see.

"He can't do that," I protest.

"But he can, unless I can prove that Ada's condition can stabilize. And more so that she benefits from your contact. I've never done this before, but I've seen men break at the loss of a loved one. I've seen them crumble, and I've seen what they turn into after these doctors get their hands on them. She will be nothing after the procedure. An empty vessel to observe the world around her, without being a part of it. She might be silent and docile but she will have lost anything that made her Ada. I don't want to see this happen Kasper, just as much as you don't. So I need you to forgo any plans you had to escape or any you are conspiring to include with her and I need you to put your trust in me fully."

He hands me the letter from Ada followed by a pen and a blank piece of paper from the inner pocket of his coat.

"She can't know," he reminds me. "This stays here."

I nod and open her letter.

Kasper,

I'm in tears as I write this. But the good kind. The kind that fall when I think of how much life has become with you in it. You have enraptured my soul with purpose, with a longing that feels both sentimental and intoxicating. Beverly and I are working hard on creating plans for the Christmas Eve Ball. When I heard we'd be visiting with Stanfield, I could barely contain my excitement. I don't know how Dr. Rosco made it happen, but I believe

HIM NOW TO BE A BLESSING GIFTED TO US BY SOMETHING GREATER IN THE COSMOS. I LIKE TO THINK GOD HAD A HAND IN IT. MAYBE SOMEWHERE IN THE UNIVERSE, OUR NAMES ARE TALKED ABOUT. MAYBE THEY SEE OUR LOVE STORY AND WANT TO BE A PART OF IT. MAYBE DR. ROSCO IS JUST AS CRAZY AS US. OR MAYBE, IT'S EVERYONE ELSE THAT'S CRAZY FOR TRYING TO STOP US. I LOVE YOU, KAS. I WILL ALWAYS LOVE YOU. COUNTING THE DAYS.

ADA

A tear falls down my cheek. I've never been a crying man, but the emotions she evokes in me are inevitable, like us.

I start writing my letter, forgetting Dr. Rosco is even in the room, so focused on what I want to say. It's a simple letter this time. Few words are all I need.

I hand the doctor the paper, this time leaving it unfolded. It's my quiet way of telling him to read it. He picks up on the hint and moves his eyes over the paper to my sloppy cursive handwriting, satisfied with what he sees. He folds it up, places it in a small envelope that he carried with him and puts it in his pocket. He reaches out his hand to shake mine, something he hasn't attempted since our first meeting. It's a gesture of trust. He's offering his trust in acceptance of mine. I stand up and offer him my hand back, a sturdy double shake with a delay of letting go while he makes eye contact with me. He walks out of the room, looking back just for a second and nodding to me in understanding.

Our outdoor time has begun and I am ushered out to where Archie, Donnie and Sheldon are walking the grounds. It's cold out today with flurries falling above us, but despite that, the fresh air is a reprieve from the staleness of the inside building. I barge in between Donnie and Archie, placing each of my arms around their neck.

"Well boys, it looks like I'm going to a ball."

CHAPTER 29

Ada

Dr. Rosco and I just finished our therapy session and he has given me Kasper's letter. I can't wait to open it but I want to do so in private. I'm so distracted by the excitement that while I'm heading back towards my room, I bump right into Dr. Wilson, dropping the letter. He picks it up and analyzes it for a moment, refraining from giving it back to me.

"What is this, Thompson?"

"It's a letter, sir."

"I can see that. Why is it in your possession?" he asks, knowing damn well the answer.

"It's for me, Doctor. May I please have it back?"

He smiles at me sinisterly, then puts the envelope in front of me and rips it in half. It feels like my heart is ripping along with it. I had been looking forward to that letter for the last two weeks. Those words are keeping Kasper alive for me. I need them. He can see the hurt in my eyes and satisfaction grows in his. I've always disliked Dr. Wilson, but now, I loathe him.

He places the envelope in the outside pocket of his white coat and walks away from me. I want to scream at him, to knock him over the head with my fist that is so tightly held that I feel my nails biting into my skin, leaving half moons behind. But I know it won't do both Kasper and I any good. I have to stay calm. I have to stay present in my mind. Christmas is close and soon, Kas will be dancing me across the floor. Those temporary moments of escape will be with him this time.

"Oh Ada, there you are! Guess what we just got in? The dress donations are here. I didn't want to sort through the boxes without you. We need to rack them which means we get first pick. Come on now!" Beverly says, pulling me towards the storage closet down the hall.

When we walk into the storage room, there are several boxes of pre worn dresses donated by the church. I haven't had a new piece of clothing in quite some time, so being able to pick a new dress is something I've been looking forward to. Even if it isn't exactly new, it's still new to me. The first dress I pick up is quite large. Though it's a beautiful deep red colour, it's not quite my style, nor would I ever get it to fit me.

The next one I pull out is an olive green gown that is a full sleeve with a high neckline and a band of fabric cinching it at the waist. I hold it up to me and realize it is far too long both in the sleeves and length.

"Isn't that one lovely," Beverly comments.

Beverly is a bit taller than me so I hand her the dress instead to look at.

I see a bit of gold material sticking out of one of the boxes that catches my eye. I pull the shiny gold fabric out of the box and know right there and then that I've found my dress. It looks to be something a bit older, maybe from the nineteen-thirties, but it's stunning nonetheless. Made of what looks to be gold brocade fabric, it has a dipped neckline that even further dips in the back with small gathered puff sleeves on the shoulders. There's a wrap of fabric crossing over the bust on each side to meet in the back with a small bustle. The gown is nearly floor length and holding it up to me, I know it'll be perfect. This dress was meant to find me. There's an elegance about it that I know Kasper will drool over and I can't wait to see the look on his face when he sees me in it.

I immediately take it to my room and hide it in the back of my wardrobe away from prying eyes and hands and head back to the storage room to continue sorting the rest of the dresses for the other women.

Tomorrow, we'll bring them into the rec room and let the others choose their dresses. It's all starting to feel real, that this is going to happen. The butterflies in my stomach start to leave their uncomfortable presence. I want to stay in this moment and relish in the eagerness that has my body buzzing.

I walk into my room at the end of the night, trying to think positively about the day, despite Dr. Wilson's attempts to ruin it. I take the dress out of my wardrobe and pretend to dance around the room with it, gleaming in the natural moon light that only enhances the gold. A knock at my door snaps me out of my fun and I'm reminded that it's now time for sleep. I put the dress back and get into bed in my white nightgown, the one I had to sew from Kasper ripping it in the back. I look at the new stitching fondly reminiscing on that night.

Just as I'm about to close my eyes, I hear movement in my room with the subtle sounds of footsteps. I look up and don't see anyone there. I assume it's someone walking by the hall. But the air gets cold and I feel a pressure pressing down at the end of my bed. When I sit up, I pull my blankets up to my mouth, covering my inhaled scream as much as I can. Edward is sitting at the end of my bed, staring down at me, the same as when I saw him last. His eyes are eerie, real and yet so disconnected.

He speaks to me without his lips ever moving. "Be happy, Ada," his voice says, as if whispering into my ear beside me. He smiles slightly, the two ripped pieces of the envelope falling from his hand to land on my bed.

I look down at them in surprised confusion and then back at him. He nods to me, then stands up and walks towards the door, walking through it as if it were opened even though it's solidly shut. He just disappears into nothing.

I grab the two pieces of paper inside the ripped envelope and put them together to read the message Kasper left for me.

> ADA,
>
> LOVE WILL FIND A WAY —
>
> — THROUGH PATHS WHERE WOLVES FEAR TO PREY.
>
> KASPER

Lord Byron. I've read this before. It's in one of my books. I hold the two pieces to my chest and sink into my bed, kissing each one of them. "Thank you Edward," I whisper.

I repeat to myself once more as I close my eyes. *Love will find a way.*

CHAPTER 30

Kasper

I've played it over and over again in my head. Today's the day. Christmas Eve was never something I'd get excited about but this year is different. Fortunately for us, donations were given for some more appropriate clothing. Stanfield has always let us wear our own outside clothes unlike some institutions that have uniforms. They wanted us to have a semblance of normalcy inside these walls even if there is nothing normal about it. I, however, came here as a prisoner, not self admitted and not sent by family, so I had little but the clothes on my back and a few pieces I was given. Luckily I'm now the temporary owner of a dark brown wool suit. It's a bit short in the legs by an inch or so, and the sleeves only just reach to where they should be with no room to spare, and there's a small patch on the back shoulder where the fabric is different, but it'll do.

The anticipation is nearly killing me. Sheldon and Donnie both got called in the lottery, but Archie didn't. However, we're not letting that stop us from sneaking him in. There's no way we're celebrating this without him. We've already worked out a plan with a little negotiating with the kitchen staff, one particular staff member who has an eye for Donnie.

"All right gentlemen. If everyone could please return to your rooms. The hall is in need of being set up for today's festivities. For those of you attending, you must be ready for fifteen hundred hours, dressed in your proper attire. For those of you not attending, you will look forward to tomorrow's Christmas feast instead."

"Nurse, will you be there tonight?" Archie asks nurse Barker, the one he's been crushing on for months now.

"I will be, but you won't. Your name wasn't called, isn't that right?"

"You were listening for it then, weren't you?" he winks. "Don't worry, I'll be there. I've switched with someone else."

"Well then you better make sure your name is on that list, otherwise, you aren't getting in. No breaking the rules now." She points her finger toward Archie and then to me and Donnie, who puts his hands up in surrender.

We get back to our main recreational quarters that overlook the property and out the window in the distance, I see a small bus pulling up. My stomach tightens knowing Ada might be in there. They pull up to the front of the building where I see Dr. Rosco exiting the bus followed by a blond woman and a much taller one with red hair, brighter than Archie's.

"She's a looker!" one of the men says. "I'll be dancing with her tonight."

His comment catches the attention of the other men, who rush over to the window, blocking my view to see those exiting the bus. Donnie is pushing in front of me to get a look for himself and by the time I get a proper view out the window again, the bus is empty, with two men remaining, carrying a tree inside the facility.

"Your woman there, Kas?" Archie asks.

"I couldn't tell. You fuckers were blocking the view."

"Ah, relax. You'll see her soon enough," Donnie says, patting my shoulder, his own strength more than he's aware of with each tap.

It's only 1:00 p.m and we've got a couple hours to go of being stuck in this damn suffocating room, while a bunch of sexually deprived men discuss the women they saw.

"Terrible idea if you ask me," Sheldon says. "They say we're crazy. I'd say putting together the male and female mentally insane population is just as ludacris. We'd better be on our best behavior or else they'll never let us do this again."

"Well boys, I've got a date. Time to prepare, I think," Archie comments.

"If by date you mean that nurse who would gladly electrocute your brain if given the chance, good luck to you," Donnie teases.

"Speak for yourself. She'll be taking my pants off at the end of the night. Just you wait," Archie says back.

Donnie laughs "Yea, to tuck your ass into bed. Not to join you!"

"I wonder what kind of food they're serving. I'm famished," Sheldon announces.

Archie looks off to the side as if trying to remember something. "When I was a young lad, my ma used to make us turkey soup. She'd save up all year for it. We didn't have much meat but we had that turkey soup and I tell ya, what I wouldn't do to have it again. My brother and I were a bit of a handful for her growing up and Da was messed up from the first war and God knows none of us deserved it, but she always made that soup. And if we were really lucky, we'd get an orange on Christmas Day. D'ya know, I don't remember the last time I had an orange. But I can still taste it. Funny, isn't that?"

"Memories have a way to encapsulate all our senses," I reply.

"D'ya have any memories from Christmas's past? When you were a boy, that is," Archie asks me.

"Just one. We were poor growing up. Didn't have much aside from the clothes on our back. My first Christmas with my aunt, and the only Christmas I had with my cousin Thomas was a good one. We were close, him and I. It was also the only Christmas I was given a gift. It was a hand me down one but it helped me learn how to read better. I wasn't much of a reader but I always wanted to, so my aunt and cousin got me a book. A poetry book."

"Who was it by?" Donnie asks.

"Tennyson," I tell him.

"I don't know much about that. Never was much of a reader," Archie admits.

I repeat the words so ingrained into my memory from Tennyson. "Half-light, half-shadow, let my spirit sleep. They never learnt to love who never knew to weep."

***

Anticipation slows down time. The minutes tick by agonizingly, waiting to be called down for the Christmas Ball. All dressed up with no place to go except within these walls where once my prison will soon become a mirage of escape.

"You handsome devil you, Archer. I think you might actually have a chance with that nurse," I say.

"You think? Well if you'll excuse me, gentlemen. I have a very important meeting to attend," he winks. "See you there."

Archie leaves and Donnie and I wait by the door with sweaty palms, hardly being able to stand still.

"Christ, I've never seen you such a wreck," he says to me.

Sheldon walks in at Donnie's comment, slapping me on the back. "Better catch your breath there first, Kas. You're going to pass out on us before you even get there."

Fuck, I'm nervous. It doesn't feel real that she's actually here, that she is inside the very walls that have been keeping me from her.

A second bus came by about twenty minutes ago and I didn't see Ada get out. I'm starting to wonder if something happened. Maybe she came in the earlier bus. Maybe she didn't make it at all and I'm about to have the worst Christmas yet.

A guard comes over to the door. "Alright gentlemen. If I call your name, you may exit the room and head into the hall. For all others, you'll remain here in the meantime. Games will be provided to keep you occupied for the afternoon."

He starts reading the list alphabetically by last name. "Abbott, Andrews, Azerman, Bailey, Bennington, Borden, Clarner..."

I exit the room and don't wait for Donnie and Sheldon. I've got my mind on one thing and one thing only.

There's more staff on duty than I've ever seen but I don't blame them considering they are mixing up the sexes. When I walk into the main room as more men follow in behind me, I see the group of women split into various smaller groups, chatter amongst them echoing in the large space. There's a large Christmas tree at the back centre of the wall in between two windows, lit up with falling silver tinsel, and red bows covering it. Tables are lined up against the closest wall to me, with green garland and holly, holding food and refreshments. There are more tables set up on the far left and right sides of the room with an area empty in the middle for dancing. The tables are draped in red cloth with centerpieces of pinecones and evergreen branches. A gramophone is set up just beside the entrance door with instrumental Christmas music playing.

It looks amazing in here but I don't let myself get distracted long enough. I look around the room, searching for Ada, moving around others in the crowd that has started to merge with patients from both facilities.

Across the room, standing by the tree is Dr. Rosco, who's talking to a woman. Her auburn hair is pinned in an updo, accentuating the drop in fabric on her backside. He notices me and mumbles some words and the woman he is talking to slowly turns around. Her honey brown eyes widen and fill with tears and she runs towards me as I do the same, impatiently waiting to embrace each other. It's a surreal moment when Ada and I connect. Her arms wrap around my neck and mine around her waist. The shaking of my breath feels soothed as I hold her. I inhale her scent, lift her up off the ground and twirl her around just once before I set her down and hold her face in my palms, wiping the tear that has freshly fallen down her cheek. We're both speechless. I know the guards and other staff members are watching but I don't care. I kiss her viciously, my tongue mixing with hers that I so badly want to suck into my own mouth.

"Peach," is the only word I can get out.

"Kasper, I can't believe this. Is this real? Is this all real?" she asks.

"It's real, baby. We're real." I hold her hands in mine, not ever wanting to let go.

She starts laughing. We both do, not believing that we're actually here, together.

"How are they treating you here?" she asks concerningly.

I want to assure her that I'm happy, even though the happiness here is short lived. I know she worries about me as much as I worry about her. "I'm okay. Your letters have gotten me through it. How are you doing?"

"Well, besides Dr. Wilson, who is still a complete arse, I'm okay. Dr. Rosco has been working with me and there are more good days now. I got you something, Kas."

She pulls me to where the Christmas tree is. I glance over at one of the tables to see Archie, Donnie and Sheldon sitting together. I smile at Archie, glad to see he made it in afterall. He's got a look on his face I can't quite discern. Something of pride and sorrow.

Ada dips down under the tree and grabs a small gift wrapped in brown paper.

"Roy helped me get it for you, so don't give me much credit. But I wanted you to have something. I had to get it approved by your doctor of course. They were pretty strict with us bringing in anything here."

She hands me the gift. I unwrap it to see a leather journal with a strap that wraps around the entire book, tucked in to keep the pages closed. I open it up to see Ada has written on the first page.

> *Keep writing for me, for us. One day, you'll read this journal to me, all of your words, your poems, your thoughts. Keep us alive so that one day, we may share in this together. I'll always be your Ada, in this soul, in this life, in any.*

My Ada. She's mine. I lean over and kiss her gently on the forehead and tuck the journal under my arm to free my hands. I grab a piece of tinsel from the tree and take her hand.

"I don't have a gift for you. But I do have my promise."

I take her ring finger and wrap the tinsel around it, tying it just tight enough to fit her finger without it falling off, breaking off the excess with my teeth.

"One day, I'm going to put a real ring on this finger. But it's only a symbol, because you've forever etched your name into my heart. It only beats for you now. I wish I could steal you away right now and show you how much I've missed you."

"Maybe there's a way." She steps away from me and goes to speak with Dr. Rosco, pulling him aside from his conversation with Dr. Forrester to speak in private. He eyes me down suspiciously, but then motions for me to come closer."

"What are the chances that you end up back in this hall after?" he asks, implying that he's willing to help us out.

"You have my word, and I've never gone back on my word."

"Follow me," he says, reluctantly, ushering us out into the hall. He calls one of the guards over and whispers something in his ear. The guard nods and then he pushes us into a small room to the right.

"You have fifteen minutes. Not a minute more," he says, shutting the door behind us.

Ada and I look around and start laughing.

"You and I keep finding ourselves in the most romantic of spaces," she says, taking in the large linen and supply closet we're currently in.

I'm nervous, more nervous than I've been since meeting her for the first time. I place the journal she got me on one of the shelves and bring my full attention to only her.

Our amusement with the privilege of our situation soon turns more serious, our time alone closing in on us by the second. I don't waste anymore as I run my hand through some loose strands fallen from her silky cinnamon hair. She closes her eyes to my touch and I pull her in close to me.

"Give me something to remember," she says gently against my mouth.

I run my lips slowly across hers, both faintly parting but not fully pressed. I inhale the breathe she offers me as I push her against the wall.

"You are breathtaking," I say, scrolling my eyes down her entire body, her gold gown only highlighting her eyes.

She presses her hips into me, trailing her hands down my back. I ignite our passion by kissing her deeply, my entire body in flames, my cock pressing into the wool of my pants uncomfortably. I lift the fabric of her gown up to reach my hand under, surprised to feel that she isn't wearing any panties.

"My little temptress," I whisper into her ear as I rub my two fingers around her already wet pussy.

She starts unbuttoning my shirt and pushes both that and the jacket off my body.

"Turn around," I demand. I take my bottoms off, underwear and all and unzip her dress.

We may be limited on time, but I'll be damned if I don't get to feel her entire form against mine. I pull the dress down her body, letting her step out of it and kneel down behind her, pulling her hips out and pressing my face into her glistening sex as she uses the wall for support. Inhaling her scent makes my cock jump and I'm greedy for everything she can give me. I run my tongue along her, lapping up her wetness into my mouth while she quietly moans into the action, pushing her body into my face.

I stand up, leaning against the back of her body as I push her front against the wall. I wrap my arm around her stomach and let my hand slip down, feeling the slickness between her legs. I move my wet fingers down a little further and stick two inside of her right away, not giving her a second to adjust. I want her feral and writhing into me, her pleas of desperation to be embedded into my memories.

"Oh God, Kas," she cries out. "I need you inside of me."

I pull my fingers out and slap her pussy, a sound of pleasure and surprise leaving her mouth. She pushes her ass into my cock and widens her legs for me. I do it again, harder and her head drops back.

"Please, Kasper. Fill me," she begs.

I pull her hips back slightly once more, having her press her hands against the wall and line myself up with her entrance. Rubbing it teasingly against her first, I bite her shoulder from behind and push myself into her deeply.

She moans as I hold her hips tightly, my hands digging into her flesh with a bruising grip while I fuck her unrelentingly hard and fast. She feels incredible, her wetness accompanying our noises of pleasure.

"Fuck, Ada," I say, trying not to let myself come too soon. It's been too long since I've felt this and other than my hand, there's been nothing else to soothe the ache.

I don't ease up on her and I can feel her legs starting to shake. I pull out and turn her around. I want her to face me when she comes. I move my mouth down to her pretty pink nipple and put it in my mouth, licking and nipping at it, then lift her up by her thighs, wrapping them around me while I sink into her, her back pressed against the wall. I lean into her neck and bite into her flesh, leaving teeth marks in its place before moving up to her mouth. She bites down on my lower lip and I groan in response. I continue to move in and out of her with the depth she craves.

"I'm gonna come," she pants out. I stop moving and wait for her to focus her attention back on me, her body aching with the need for release.

"Look at me."

She does so with a surrender in her gaze, with a light I've been deprived of seeing for so long.

I push into her again, my arms growing tired from this position, but I like the burning from my muscles while I hold her body against mine. I want my arms to be heavy and sore tomorrow, to think of this when they ache. I build her up again, both of us about to explode, increasing my speed as her lips part. With her eyes still focused on me, I kiss her with unabating pressure. There's only us in this room right now. Only now. Nothing outside this room exists.

"God, baby. I fucking love you," I say.

She comes undone with my words, releasing everything holding inside of her for all these months, her moans heavy, followed by mine as I come into my own release, the warmth of my come filling inside her. The pleasure feels endless, this carnal energy that's been stored inside us this whole time drawing out our orgasms, reverberating inside the walls of this small room.

Ada looks at me longingly, her eyes heavier and relaxed as her body weakens in my hold.

I gently set her down, exiting her body, watching the come drip down her inner thigh. I kneel down and lick my come upwards to gather it in my mouth and stand to press it against hers. She opens her mouth without command and takes in every drop I offer her from my tongue, tasting our combination of desire.

Someone knocks on the door, snapping us out of our moment.

We both know our time is almost over. But we'll soak up whatever we can get until they pull us apart from each other.

CHAPTER 31

Ada

We get dressed quickly, using a spare linen from the room to clean up and ready ourselves to get back into the hall. My hair is no doubt disheveled and I try to pat it down and tame the curls. Kasper zips up the back of my dress and we both nod to each other before opening the door.

We could try to escape right now, but both of us know the only chance we really stand is by trusting Dr. Rosco to keep us connected.

Kasper grabs my hand and the guard looks at us with both jealousy and indignation. We walk back into the hall and the relief that falls on Dr. Rosco across the room has me putting a small smile on my face. Kasper squeezes my hand tight and leads me over to where a few men stand. One is quite small, the other a complete polar opposite. He must be the largest man in this room. The other man is maybe around Kasper's size, perhaps a bit taller but much more slim and with red hair and pale features. He's looking at someone across the room that he can't seem to pull his eyes away from.

"There you are. Thought you got yourself sent to confinement again," the man with the red hair says.

"Confinement?" I question.

Kasper ignores the comment and introduces us. All the men look at me with smirks on their faces, the man named Archie having the biggest one of them all.

"Nice to meet you, Ada," he says, offering his hand. "We've been hearing about you every day since this guy showed up. I was starting to think this was a Romeo and Juliet kind of story."

"I thought you didn't read," Kasper says.

"I'm not completely daft. I do know a thing or two," Archie says, bumping his side body into Kaspers.

"There you are, Ada! I've been looking all over for you," Beverly exclaims.

I introduce Beverly, and Silvia soon follows in behind her, mingling with us.

"Well aren't you a tall glass of milk," Donnie says to Silvia. He then turns to Beverly.

"And you are ravishing. I think I just fell in love."

She blushes and looks down.

Donnie grabs her chin gently to lift her face back up. "Don't you dare look away from me now, sweetheart. How about you and I go have a dance?"

He pulls her off onto the dance floor area that is filling up quickly with patients, laughing and being silly.

Kasper pulls me onto the floor following their lead. "Come on angel, let's have our dance."

One dance turns into two, which turns into three. We get lost in each other's hold, not wanting to let go of this. We take a small break to get some food in us, and then we're back on the dance floor.

"Mind if I have a dance with the pretty lady?" says Archie.

Kasper looks as though he wants to say no, selfishly wanting me all to himself, but he waits for me to answer instead.

"Just one," I wink.

Kasper steps away to talk to Sheldon, not taking his eyes off me for a single second. Archie pulls me in by my waist with one arm and holds my hand with the other, still leaving ample space between us.

"He's a lucky guy you know."

"I'm not sure most would agree given our situations but I suppose we are lucky, aren't we? It's rare what we have. Do you have a woman?" I ask.

"Ah me? Nah. Maybe one day once I get out of here. That's all we can hope for in life really, to love and be loved."

"I agree. I think of all the people who have lived full lives without experiencing this. I pity them."

"Well, he's not giving up on you. I don't think it's possible. The guy could be buried deep in his grave and he'll still be trying to plan his escape. We've gotten to know each other quite well. Took a little convincing to get him to be my friend. He doesn't trust easily but when he does let you in, he's loyal to a fault, like a dog. But a protector, a savage one."

"Sounds like you're pretty loyal yourself."

"Sure. But not like him. He'll live everyday, go through hell every day if he has to, for the slightest chance that he'll one day be free of this place. Not me. I wouldn't have it in me."

The song ends and Archie pulls away, Kasper returning to me right away to take over.

"Archer's the only one who gets to dance with you today. I won't share you with anyone else."

It feels like only minutes have gone by but the room is dark with the sun in full set, the lights from the tree illuminating the space. Despite the fact we're in an asylum, there's been no major drama to compromise a future dance. If I have to wait a year to do this again, then so be it. The event has been a success.

A staff member announces the end of the ball. Names are called out to return back to rec quarters and are let out one by one until the patients that remain are only from Huberts, with the exception of Kasper.

He hasn't budged his eyes from me, even as his name is called. Though the music has stopped, in his mind it hasn't and he still dances with me, circling the middle of the room as the onlooking patients speak of us. Their voices of gossip are muffled to our ears as we are so entranced in our final moments.

"Let's go Mr. Bailey," a doctor calls to his attention.

He still doesn't budge, still not breaking his gaze from mine.

"Mr. Bailey," the doctor repeats himself and I hear Dr. Rosco call my name too.

"Say your goodbyes."

I see the pain, his forehead pinching together as Kasper's grip loosens on me. He leans in for one final kiss, long and unmoving, finally pulling away from me. My heart feels like it's breaking all over again, just as it did when the police arrested him in front of me. But there's a little shred of hope this time.

"I love you. Keep writing to me, okay?" I say, holding back the tears, a tight feeling gripping my chest as he moves away.

"I love you," is all he says in return, slowing backing away from me with the doctor, looking back twice to see me still standing and staring at him.

Once he's out of the room, I collapse down to the ground, my hands covering my face and sob. Dr. Rosco kneels down to me and rubs my back trying to comfort me.

There's so much uncertainty in our future, the doubt like a disease trying to take over my brain, but I have to be stronger this time.

"Come on, Ada. Let's get this place cleaned up."

I grab onto Dr. Rosco's wrist as he tries to stand, pausing his movement.

"Roy," I say, calling him by the name he always tells me to call him in our sessions. "Thank you."

CHAPTER 32

Kasper

Last night was the best night of sleep I've had since being placed here many months ago. Christmas day brings with it a bitter sweetness. Yesterday was a dream and today I get to reminisce on my visit with Ada, despite her absence.

"Beautiful morning, Archer," I say.

"It's still dark out."

"Yes, but what a day to be alive."

We wake up as per our usual routine, and after getting dressed, head to the hall for our breakfast.

Archer excuses himself while Donnie and I get in line for the Christmas breakfast we have been looking forward to.

Hard boiled eggs are served with black pudding, tea and canned peaches on the side that makes me smile thinking of Ada.

We sit down and eat, still no sign of Archie.

"Merry Christmas, gentleman," Dr. Forrester says with a cup of tea in his hand.

"Merry Christmas, doc," I say. "And uhhh... thank you."

He nods with a smile hinting through as he walks to another table to make his rounds.

"Where'd that red headed bastard go? Christmas morning without him? Maybe he's shagging up with that nurse finally. Wouldn't that be something?"

Dr. Forrester is called away from outside the hall by a nurse, the very nurse Archie is crushing on. Except she looks panicked, her eyes wide and her face pale. Dr. Forrester runs out of the room and I follow suit, running past the staff who watch me leave.

"Mr. Billows found him just minutes ago. On Christmas day of all days. What do we do sir?" I hear the staff say. This feeling in my gut sinks deep and sharp and every siren is going off in my head.

There's a guard blocking off the door to the storage room. Dr. Forrester notices me and the look on his face drops.

"What's going on?" I ask.

The doctor pauses, stumbling his words when he speaks, "P-please go back into the dining h-hall."

I push the guard out of the way and into the room to see Archie hanging from the ceiling in the storage room by a string of christmas lights attached to a metal pipe at the top of the room.

"Archer, FUCK! Get him down!" I grab his body and try lifting it to relieve the pressure on his neck but he's limp. "Someone fucking help me!"

The doctor comes in and places a hand on my shoulder and the guard pulls me away, another standing on the other side of him, pulling me back.

"Archer, wake up! Get him down. He'll be okay," I say, even though I know he won't.

I'm pulled out of the room, and pushed against the wall by both guards.

"Get your fucking hands off of me!" I yell. "You were supposed to help him! You weren't supposed to let him die!"

Dr. Forresters face is heavy. It's taking every ounce of control not to go over and shake him senseless, but I know it won't do anything except put me in solitary again and I need to be there for Ada. *God this fucking hurts.*

My yells attract attention and Donnie and Sheldon are standing at the door of the hall, being held back in trying to get to me.

"Dammit Archer! Fuck!" I drop down, admitting defeat, trying to slow my breathing before I burst.

"Archie was very sick, Kasper. We can only do so much for our patients. At the end of the day, they have to choose to live."

I stare at the floor by his shoes, not daring to look up. I can't face him right now. I am absolutely gutted. What was supposed to be a day of celebration has become a day of grief and I can't bear the pain of this place much longer.

"Please, put me to sleep. Give me something, please!" I plead.

"Come on, let's get you some rest." A nurse brings me into the sleeping quarters and gives me a pill of sorts. I don't care what it does as long as it makes me numb.

***

It's been a week since Archie's death. It doesn't feel real. His bed is now taken up by a new occupant, an older man who constantly hums to himself.

A day's peace is all I was offered in this hell hole. A day to be with the love of my life before death tangled its web and took Archie for its meal. The grim reaper and I have some unfinished business and when I meet him, he'll have to answer to his actions.

I've been told Dr. Rosco is waiting for me. I haven't left my bed much since Archie's death. Donnie and Sheldon are as devastated as I am. We've all been in our own head space since. I'm scared to get close to anyone. The curse is back. How many more deaths do I have to witness in this life before my own.

I walk in with my sullen face, Dr. Rosco's matching mine as I sit down. My facial hair is rough having not had a good shave all week and the circles under my eyes have darkened.

"I'm sorry to hear about your friend. I know it's already hard enough to make connections in a place like this."

I don't look at him. I just stare at the table waiting for him to change the subject.

Dr. Forrester walks in right after and stands against the wall beside me.

"This is my last visit here, Kasper," Dr. Rosco tells me.

I look up at him, worry coursing through me. He's my bridge to Ada.

Dr. Forrester speaks next. "You're being transferred, Mr. Bailey. I'm afraid given the circumstances, it's no longer in your best interest to stay here."

"I don't understand. Where am I going?"

"To a different place, more suitable. It's a smaller environment, both men and women, though the wards are separated the same. But we feel that it would be better for you long term," Dr. Forrester confirms.

"Okay, but what about Ada?"

"Ada is fine. You're being transferred to Huberts II sister home. It's closer and I have a good relationship with the director there," Dr. Rosco assures me.

This could be a good thing. I'll be closer to Ada. The doctor has good connections. We can make this work.

"When do I leave?"

"In two days time. You'll have a room with three other patients, so it will be quieter. But you're expected to be an ideal patient when you're there. You know how it runs, similar to Huberts I. No nonsense."

"Of course," I agree.

"Good. You have a couple friends to say goodbye to I believe?" Dr. Forrester reminds me.

I haven't been one to make many friends in this life, but the ones I made here have given me some good memories that I'll gladly take with me. I hope wherever Archie went after his death, it was far from here. Perhaps there's turkey soup and the company of his ancestors.

Donnie and Sheldon's friendship will be missed and if either of them are lucky enough to get out of here someday, I hope they come to visit me.

"I am sorry for your loss, Mr. Bailey, but I do believe this is a solution that will benefit you in the long run." Dr. Forrester smiles subtly at me and walks out, Dr. Rosco now standing up to do the same.

"Thank you for putting your trust in me, Kasper."

"Thank you for being a man I could trust."

CHAPTER 33

Ada

Yesterday was everything and I'm holding onto that. I'm holding onto every moment he held me, every moment he kissed me, every moment he caressed my skin, every fraction of a second when we were one, when we were sane.

The day is still dark, the morning new and our wake up call has not begun. I take this as an opportunity to reawaken my senses in the best of ways, thinking about the remnants of Kaspers passion still inside of me. I lower my hand to lift my nightgown from under my covers, gliding my hand up my thigh and press into my lower lips, parting them to feel the wetness gathered. I rub it around gently, pretending it's Kasper's hand instead of mine.

"Touching yourself is a sin," I hear a woman's voice in the distance say.

She's sitting at my vanity in the dark, her face not visible, just the shadow of her until she steps up and walks over to me.

Nurse Arden.

"You mention sin like you are worthy of praise, but I believe your reputation would counter that comment, you complete hypocrite."

She laughs in an exhale. "Dr. Rosco is leaving, you know. He won't be here to have your back anymore. Dr. Wilson has much better plans for you. Don't worry. I'll be here to make sure you're well taken care of."

Her smile is menacing and her eyes turn white. *Not again.*

I bring my lower palms to my eyes to rub them, hoping to clear the imagery from my vision.

"I hope you enjoyed last night, because you'll never see Kasper again. Dr. Wilson will make sure of that. He'll wither away behind walls the same as you, and soon enough you won't even care. You won't even remember who Kasper is."

Spiders are crawling out of her mouth again and her teeth turn black and sharp.

"Get out!" I yell.

She walks away but not out the door. Instead, into my wardrobe. She grabs the gold dress I wore yesterday and rips it down the front.

"Stop!" I yell, standing up to walk towards her.

But she doesn't. Instead, she reaches towards the back of my wardrobe and finds the untouched book with the poem's I salvaged from the old books that were previously destroyed, as well as Kasper's letters. The piece of tinsel he wrapped around my finger is between pages and with one rip, she tears down the spine of the book, the piece of tinsel falling to the ground. She takes the letters and goes to rip them and every part of me wants to lunge at her, the same as I had before. But I know how this works. This is what she wants. Instead, I run out into the hall and yell for help!"

"Please, she's destroying my things, help, please!"

Nurse Bentley, the night duty nurse, comes over immediately and enters the room, turning the light on to see Nurse Arden standing there with my letters in her hand.

"You're not on this ward. Why are you in here?" Nurse Bentley asks.

"I heard her yelling and walked in to find her destroying her things again. Thought I would put a stop to it."

"She's lying," I say through clenched teeth. "Why would I destroy the only things I hold so dear to me?"

The spiders on her face re-enter her mouth and her eyes turn to their normal shade, her teeth, to their normal shape.

"I'll take it from here," says Nurse Bentley.

Nurse Arden smiles and nods, leaving the room but dropping my letters on the ground in the process of her exit. I get on my knees and start to pick things up. The other nurse helps until everything is put back in place. I can't find the piece of tinsel though. I run my eyes along the floor and through the gathered pages but it's nowhere to be found. Giving up on the search with the sun starting to rise, I take that as my cue to get ready, using the lavatory and getting myself dressed for the day.

Breakfast is called for soon after and I head to the hall, but am called away by Dr. Rosco before I can get there.

"I thought I might have a word with you. It won't take long. My office please, Ada."

I follow him down the long hall, enter the small office and have a seat. Instead of him taking the seat across from me, he takes the one next to me, angling his chair to face me. I do the same.

"There's something important that has come up that I didn't want to wait in telling you. I'm leaving, Ada. I'm being transferred to a different facility that I think will be more suitable for the kind of care I wish my patients to experience. The head of psychology is retiring and I've been voted in to take his place as the front running doctor there, an opportunity I wish not to pass up. Dr. Wilson and I don't exactly see eye to eye here and it's best for me to find a place I can finish my career off at. I've had a lot of changes over these past couple years as you know and I need to set some roots again. I thought I could do that here, but I was wrong."

So Nurse Arden was right. He's leaving, which means I won't see Kasper anymore. The dread that is running through me is palpable, my face showing every line of concern.

"This was a difficult decision for me. Of course I don't want to leave everyone here, but I feel there's a larger mission at hand for me that I can't accomplish here."

"But, Roy, you said –"

He cuts me off and takes my hands in his.

"Ada, I spoke with Dr. Wilson when this position came up. He was quick in agreeing to see me gone from here, but I made a deal with him. I would only leave on the condition I could transfer you with me as a patient. The facility I'm moving to has agreed. You will be leaving Huberts with me in two weeks time. They are making all the arrangements. The set up is a little different and you will have bedmates, but I'm told the facility is better run, in better condition and with good staff that are willing to work with you in a way that is productive for your healing."

"I'll be leaving my friends though."

"Yes," he confirms, "but you'll make new friends and you can still write to Beverly here if you wish."

"I don't know. It's a lot of change."

"Yes, it is. But holding you in the same building where your mother once stayed is a cruel thing. You've seen too much here. It's not the right place for you to be anymore. Nurse Bentley filled me in on this morning. I know you didn't do it, Ada. Nurse Arden has her own agenda here, one I will not have any control over when I leave."

"Okay," I say hesitantly. "I'll go. With you."

"Good. It's the right decision."

"I suppose you haven't let me down yet."

"And I hope to never have to," he replies.

"I'll still be able to correspond with Kasper from there?" It's the only question running through my mind that really matters.

"I will still make sure that you two are able to communicate."

The reassurance eases my mind. We finish out the details of our conversation, mostly discussing the arrangements here until then. He tells me Nurse Arden will be taking a small vacation until our departure and that I am to continue therapy sessions and a regular schedule once we make the move.

After we're done, I'm excused and head back to the hall to get breakfast in me and tell Beverly of my departure. She's disappointed but is happy for me to leave this place and most importantly, to get away from Dr. Wilson. Hopefully whoever replaces Dr. Rosco will be just as kind hearted as him.

Two more weeks until I start fresh. I just wish my fresh start was with Kasper. I've called this place home for as long as I've escaped from it in my mind. There's fear in the unfamiliar, but this time there's also hope.

CHAPTER 34

Kasper

This place feels like a vacation compared to Stanfield, though I do miss the boys back there. Thankfully, I've made some new friends here. My one bedmate is named Victor. He's close to my age and is in here for stress related disturbances. He's a bit neurotic and has a routine of things, like shutting the light off three times before bed, or making sure he eats his food in a clockwise direction, but otherwise, he's been a good bloke to talk to.

The other men in our room are older. One is named William. He's been here longer than any patient but the rumours as to why are not yet clear. However, he is a wise old man and always has a story for us of some sort. Sometimes I'll fall asleep to his tales. I think he knows it calms Victor, but it has the same effect on me.

The last guy in my room is here for addiction. He's a volunteer case and has been in and out for the past four years. His wife said she'd leave him for good if he didn't fix himself this time. He turned to the drink after the first war. They lost their only son, a pilot during the second war and his drinking got worse since. Sometimes I hear him crying at night. Sometimes I want to cry too.

Ada keeps me strong though. Dr. Rosco is coming today to visit, I've been told, and I'm looking forward to receiving a letter from my girl.

The rules here are a little more lax. The therapy is much more talk based except for a hydrotherapy room where we get to soak in warm water for relaxation, unlike the cold water experience we had at Stanfield. The outdoor space has the promise of beautiful gardens, which I'm told we are to tend to once the spring hits. They allow us to grow our own vegetables to help with the cost of food, and we're given duties here to keep our minds occupied. They even have a small library that I've volunteered to help out in a few times a week. The women and the men here are kept separate during the nighttime hours, but during the day, we are gathered in the same spaces. It's a little more unconventional than Huberts I. I think they made this place different on purpose, an experiment in itself to see how the patients would fare in comparison to a more traditional approach.

The staff here also seem happier. That makes all the difference.

Meal duties are alternated between patients. We are each assigned shifts to help out in the kitchen to wash dishes and to take turns serving the food here as well.

"Dr. Rosco will see you now," Nurse Walsh tells me. "He is waiting for you in the library."

I follow her down until I reach the larger room towards the back of the building on the first floor. There's no one in here at the moment, or at least I think so, until I see someone behind a bookshelf, looking through what I know to be the fiction section. I only see the edge of a dress poking out from the side of the large shelf, but when she pulls a book out, I get just a hint of her hair colour. I seem to see Ada everywhere. Even though I know it's not her, I enjoy pretending it is, even for a short glimpse in time.

"Ah, there you are," Dr. Rosco says behind me, pulling my attention away. I turn towards him, facing away from the woman to greet him and shake his hand.

He looks over my shoulder and smiles.

"Kasper?" I hear my name. I know that voice.

I turn around and the woman standing there drops the book in her hand and lights up like a firefly.

"Ada?"

Dr. Rosco pats me on the shoulder, then pushes me gently towards her.

"What are you doing here?" I ask. "How did you–"

"What are *you* doing here?" she asks me back. I'm so very confused and yet elated despite it. But I don't wait a second longer to answer or be answered before my mouth is on hers, pulling her into me and kissing her with the longing I've had since seeing her last. She sinks into me for a second, allowing herself to enjoy this moment, before she breaks free and starts laughing.

"I don't understand!" she says, looking at Dr. Rosco behind me.

"I think perhaps we should sit down for this," he suggests, leading us to a set of facing floral sofas at the front of the library. There's a small elongated table between us. Dr. Rosco takes one side and Ada and I the other, wrapping my arm around her.

"Welcome home," he starts. "Ada. You will be staying in the woman's ward next to Kasper's ward. He's been here for almost two weeks now. I will be overseeing your cases from here on out. There will be privileges based on good behaviour, but those will be revoked if any problems surface. You will have the opportunity to see each other during the day, but nighttime is still spent in separate quarters, no exceptions. There are rules you will follow and if you break them, I'm accountable to answer to them. The board is aware of this unique situation and should you find yourselves creating problems from this arrangement, they will not hesitate to make the necessary changes. I want to be clear that I had to pull some serious strings to make this happen. Do not take advantage of my kindness."

We are both in shock, neither of us speaking. I'm holding her hand and gripping it for dear life.

"Is this real?" she asks "Tell me I'm not seeing this as some hallucination."

"No Ada, this is real." He gets my attention next. "Kasper, you know this place well enough by now. Why don't you and Nurse Walsh escort Ada upstairs, give her a proper tour of the grounds while I get situated myself. I'll see you both at the dinner hour."

He gets up to leave, calling in the nurse, but I stop him for a second before he fully exits.

"Thank you, Roy," I say, with a tear in my eye I'm holding in.

He lays his hand on my shoulder and looks at me to soak up all my gratitude, not saying a word in the process before he leaves the room.

I spend the next hour and half showing Ada around, still in disbelief that she's here, that we get to be together. It might not be conventional, but it's our story, and nothing about us has ever been normal. I introduce her to some of my friends and she meets her new bedmates. Luckily, I know the women she's with and she should be in good hands.

We spend the afternoon catching up in the main recreation room and hardly take our eyes off each other, but there's more tension growing between us minute after minute. I need her. I also don't want to break the rules just hours after our reunion.

"Oh you two," Ms. Penny says, one of Ada's new bedmates. She's gotta be in her fifties, but you can tell by her face she's been through hard times.

"Off you go now. They won't look for you if you're careful. Nurses here can turn a blind eye when needed if you know what I mean."

"I don't know what you mean," Ada says, bashfully. She knows damn well what Ms. Penny means.

"Room's empty. Nobody be looking for you. Just keep your voic-es down."

Say no more. I take Ada by the hand and lead her down the hall. The staff watches us and I slow down our walk, looking casual. Halfway down the hall, we bump into Dr. Rosco.

"Where are you two getting on to," he asks.

"I was just getting settled into my room and I thought Kasper could answer some questions I had about the routine here. Would that be okay, Dr. Rosco?" Her sweet eyes open up, her expression of innocence not fooling the good doc.

"Well, dinner is in an hour. You both better be on time," he says, walking away.

I rush Ada down the remainder of the hall and walk into her room, closing the door behind us.

Her bed is away from the door, not visible through the glass on the top and she immediately pushes me onto the bed, straddling me.

"Now Mr. Bailey. Seeing as we're going to be seeing a lot more of each other now, I think it's best if we set some ground rules." She moves off me for a second, slipping off her panties and climbs back on me, undoing my trousers. She pulls them down just slightly enough to release my hardened cock from my pants.

"What kind of rules would those be, Ms. Thompson?"

She leans in to kiss me, grinding up against my length. "Well, for starters, I'm no longer Ms. Thompson. We might not be able to get married by law, but I take you, Mr. Bailey, as my own, my partner, the love of my life, in sickness and insanity for all of time, until death parts for us to walk together into new worlds."

She sinks down slowly onto my cock, rocking her body gently back and forth to deepen our connection.

"I'm Mrs. Bailey to you now. And you're my Mr. Bailey. Only mine."

I moan into her mouth as she fully takes me inside her.

"I, Jude Kasper Bailey, promise to love you in all your forms, in all your perfect delusions, for in this life and in the next, where our ghosts walk together for as long as our souls exist. God, Ada. You're perfect for me."

She continues moving her hips, which I grab onto, gripping into the flesh beneath her dress.

"Kasper. We won."

I kiss her, running my tongue over hers, pulling her body close into me, her chest against mine as I flip her over onto her back, taking over while still inside her. I pump into her harder and she bends her knees into her body in response, wanting to feel me even deeper.

"We won, baby," I repeat.

A bridge, one I got to cross.

I lift her leg over my shoulder and pump into her harder. She tries to cover her mouth to silence her moans but I move her hand away and pin it down against the mattress.

"No, peach. I wanna hear every sound out of your mouth."

"Kasper, they'll hear. I'm gonna —"

Her head tilts backwards and she arches her back as she loses control. The sight of her undoes me, but I want this to last. I want to be inside her all fucking day, nothing but our passion being heard in these walls and though I know we're limited on time today, at least I know we have tomorrow.

I turn her over, having her lay flat on her stomach and enter her from behind, my body entirely pressed into her. I wish we were naked so I could feel her soft smooth skin on mine, but I'll take this. I'll take whatever I can get of her. She's clenching onto the pillow as I fuck her harder, pushing her ass up into me. I move her hair away from her neck and breathe in her scent, flicking my tongue just under her ear before biting onto her lobe.

She reaches her arm back to my thigh, digging her nails into me sharply. The pain pushes me to the edge. I gently grab her hair by the base of her head, pulling her head back just enough so I can better reach her lips and give a couple more powerful thrusts as I release my warm come inside of her.

We don't stay in this moment long. We know at any second someone could come in, but it's the thrill of being caught that adds to the excitement of our forbidden passion.

I clean her up with the handkerchief I have in my pocket and put her panties in there to replace it.

"I believe those belong to me," she argues.

"What's yours is mine. Isn't that right, Mrs. Bailey?" I wink.

We sit on her bed for a moment longer, staring at each other as if one of us will disappear before our eyes if we look away.

Nurse Camden walks in, reminding me it's time for dinner set up. It's my night tonight to help out and I excuse myself, bringing Ada's hand up to my mouth to kiss it lightly as I walk out. But I stop in my tracks when a glint of something shiny catches in my periphery. I look down at the floor and at the edge of one of the bed posts, where the sun is reflecting, I see a small piece of silver tinsel.

Ada must have dropped this when she was... I stop myself, realizing Ada hasn't unpacked yet. I've been keeping her too distracted. I turn around to show her the piece of tinsel in my hand and her forehead scrunches with confusion at first.

She tilts her head slightly. "Where did you find that? I haven't seen that in weeks. How did you... well, how did you get that?"

"Maybe it fell out of your pocket or something," I suggest.

"I don't have any pockets." She walks over to me and holds the piece of tinsel between her fingers, feeling the smoothness and just smiles at it.

"Don't worry, darling. I'll get you a real ring soon."

"I don't need a ring, Kasper. I just need you." She kisses me then sits back down on her bed, holding the tinsel in her hand.

"Might be a good time to unpack," Nurse Camden suggests.

Ada nods and I blow her a kiss before leaving for the kitchen.

I'm pinching myself with a permanent smile stuck on my face. I might be a crazy bastard, but I'm the happiest one in the world.

CHAPTER 35

Roy

11 MONTHS LATER

I've made a lot of mistakes in my life. I should have been more supportive of Anna and the man she chose. I should have spent more time with my girls. My work was my priority. Broadmoor didn't leave much time for anything else and I didn't give my wife the attention she needed after our daughter's deaths. I was too busy trying to distract myself from the pain of which my wife only demanded to be set free from. My wife's grief was experienced alone in a dark room with no comfort to be found from the man she should have shared it with. I have to live with her decision and the ones I made before it all came crashing down, but what I won't live with anymore is bearing witness to the suffering that is indisputably caused by the separation of two souls. If this is my way to repent, then so be it.

I watch Ada and Kasper from a distance, the sounds of classical music roaming through the halls, the same as it does every morning when they wake early, just to see that they are still there, living and breathing together. They dance in the empty rec room, swaying and laughing and kissing and sometimes I come in early to bask in their happiness for a few moments before the day truly begins. This is why

I chose to do what I did, why I needed to make this story theirs and not anyone else's.

Ada still suffers from hallucinations, but her episodes are few and far between and he's there to help her through them. She hasn't fallen back into a full psychosis and though she'll never live a normal life, she'll have roots, if only within him on these grounds.

Kasper has kept up his good behavior and found friendship that he would never have given a chance to before her. They spend all day together except when they are off on their own duties or in therapy. When night falls, they sneak off, diving into the thralls of passion in the storage room. Most of us just laugh it off at this point.

Nothing about them should make sense to the outside world, but here, they get to be free. It's the strangest, most beautiful case I've ever been a part of, and yet the crazy part of it all is that even the most normal of us will never get to experience such a love as theirs.

Of course what doesn't get understood always makes headlines. Rumours soon spread about love found at Huberts II, and the papers quickly picked up the story, connecting the dots with Kasper's arrest and the tumultuous days after, in which they were separated. It was good publicity for the facility who started to welcome tours on the grounds from the upper class who wanted to see just how progressive of a facility we were. It worked so well, that Huberts original home started to adapt some of the same practices, having had a much lower success rate in patient recovery in comparison to its sister home.

Dr. Wilson, I've been notified, has just announced his retirement. Rumours say the decision was forced due to his push back regarding the recent changes and the nature of his activities with a certain staff member, one who I've been told has also been let go from her duties at Huberts.

We live in a world that is the furthest thing from normal. Yet we are required to pretend we belong, silencing our cries, adapting to our new reality. Yet those who do not conform to the confines of this world, who break out of the box are simply mislabelled, mistreated, misrepresented in a society so full of people pretending they are okay. Because if they are not, if there is any part of their existence that strays from the ordinary, they end up here and there, in places like Stanfield and Broadmoor and Huberts.

But the truth is, we're all a bit mad. The real exception of madness is that of which is love.

Epilogue - The Beginning

Kasper

12 Years Later

Ada and I had a beautiful life together. It wasn't the life we both pictured when we met all those years ago, but it was the life we were chosen for, and there wasn't a day gone by where I wasn't grateful for it.

Each day we spent the same, the routine of our lives becoming our comfort. The stories we made were written in the laugh lines on our faces, in the slight greys of our hair, and in the pages of our books.

I had almost twelve more years with Ada. Twelve more than I ever thought I would when I was taken from her. But Dr. Rosco told me to trust him, and I held that trust within us for our lifetime, a trust that has turned into a lasting friendship.

I'm a free man. I've done my time and stayed longer voluntarily to be with her, but I know it's time for us to leave this place.

I wander into the empty halls. It's 3:00 a.m and I follow my senses into the rec hall, drawn to the full moon out the main window. It's a wonder each time I see it, each time we used to pull our chairs up and just watch it for hours until we were lulled into sleep.

I wait for her again tonight. I have every night for the last two weeks but yet I have found myself alone in the flesh.

They said it was an infection that got into her blood. I tried to hold onto her. I tried so damn hard to hold onto her, but I couldn't and neither could she. But I know she's still here. I can feel her. I can feel when the room gets chilled and when my hands start to prickle because I know hers are on it and I can almost feel her breath by my face at night.

We haven't left this place yet, but we will. I can feel it coming and I'm not fighting it. Her ashes stay with me beside my bed. One day, mine will be mixed with hers and set free outside these walls. I'm drawn back to the final days of my first life, waiting for death to come get me. I can almost feel the building around me rumble, right before it falls.

Tears cloud my vision and then I hear it, music. The gramophone plays Brahms, her favourite composer, the one we first danced to in here. I stand up and look around the room but don't see anyone.

"Ada?" I say to myself.

We made a vow that whoever left this world first would wait, that we would haunt each other until our final breaths. She kept her word.

I turn back to the window, and there she is, sitting in her chair, looking at the moon.

I blink a few times but she's still there. I sit down across from her, my heart beating through my chest followed by a sharp pain in my head. I close my eyes for a second until the pain dissipates and then a calmness falls over me and she looks at me. There are no words exchanged, but I feel a warm sensation drift over my body, one I'm familiar with. She stands up and puts her hand out for me to hold.

"Our bridge, my love," she says, her lips softly turning up into a smile.

I hold her hand and can feel it truly for the first time in weeks.

I look back as we walk to see my body slouched in the chair, my face pale, my lips blue. She gives me a second to take it in. I turn towards her in understanding and we move through the hall, down the stairs to the front entrance. No one stops us. It's just us. We move through the doors without them opening and when we step outside, the moon looks even brighter, a light emitting from it that travels all the way down to the path in front of us.

"Where should we go next?" she says, taking a step into the edge of the light. I follow, holding her hand tighter.

"To new worlds."

ACKNOWLEDGMENTS

Writing a book isn't just something I wanted to do. It was something I needed to do. When that creative energy runs through me so actively, it's a cathartic experience to finally be able to get out all the thoughts that have been brewing inside my head.

Thank you to each and every one of you that has supported my need for creativity over the years, and to those that have supported my continuous writing after the debut of my first novel. Thank you for the encouragement to keep going because you believed in me as much as I did in myself.

Thank you to my family for supporting my dream, even in the toughest of days. To my husband for his unwavering love. It is because of you that I understand the obsession of love.

To my wonderful team of beta readers, Melissa, Deni, Jessica, Rob, and my mother for being the first to read this story and offer their insights and adoration.

To my editor Brittany, who was a great support during the final phases to get the last draft in tip top shape.

A special thank you to Kim for not only seeing my vision through but surpassing my expectations with the beautiful cover art.

I could not have done this without the wonderful team beside me. Finally, thank you to my readers for stepping inside my head for a little while to experience a bit of insanity along the journey that was Kasper and Ada. I love you all!

About The Author

A.H. King is a Canadian author that lives both in the light and dark, between a fictional world and the real one. Always trying to find the balance of life and never settling for a less than magical existence, she is endlessly pursuing the next dream that awakens her soul. When she isn't writing her latest inspiration, she can be found hiking in the forest to smell her favourite cedar trees or wandering in the cemetery, absorbing history for her curious mind. She has had many titles in life but her heart beats strongest when she is creating. She enjoys the spooky side of things and always has a peppermint tea on hand. She has no five year plan, just today, embracing each moment, each word, each story that finds its way on the paper in front of her.

You can find A.H. King on Instagram & Tiktok
@a.h.king.author
as well as on Goodreads.
Contact: a.h.king.author@gmail.com

If you'd like to leave a review, I would so much appreciate it. Reviews go a long way for indie authors.
Thank you!

Printed in Dunstable, United Kingdom

68241630R00139